LOST
AND
FOUND

KEVIN C. GARDNER

atmosphere press

For Joan, Gordy, and Matt.
I sure wish you guys were here to see this.

NEWPORT MORNING GAZETTE

Overnight Violence Claims Three
A fourth in critical condition

Newport – The sleepy bedroom community of Newport woke this morning to the shocking news of the overnight deaths of three more of their neighbors. Police, stopping at the country home of prominent local Presbyterian minister, T. Whitman Earle, discovered four victims. Police have confirmed that three of the victims were found dead at the scene and a fourth was found unresponsive and was rushed by Mercy Flight to Strong Memorial Hospital in Rochester. While the identities of the dead are being withheld pending notification of the next of kin, unconfirmed sources report that one of the victims, the lone survivor, is fiction writer, Arn Maxwell. Maxwell, a native of Newport, is best known for his first novel, "Outside the Dreams," and more recently for his well-publicized marital, and financial problems. Citing the need to keep the details of the on-going investigation confidential, Newport police chief, John Maynard Munger refused to comment on the possibility that the overnight violence might be related to the rash of recent suspicious deaths in the community.

ONE

Hands deep in the pockets of my Levi's, face pointing into the steady northwest wind, I stood on the large flat rock that was the end of the pier. The view hadn't changed. It had been fifteen years, but this was the place. My happy place. Standing on this rock, at the end of the Oak River west pier, looking out over Lake Ontario, the view was spectacular. To the east was a stately, tree-lined, lakefront community, and Saunders Point, with its 150-year-old sandstone lighthouse formally known as U. S. Lighthouse #1475. The east pier was already filling up with men, some with their families, all laden with poles and tackle, all looking to bring home the 'big one'. Also, to the south, looking up the harbor, pleasure craft of every style, along with a modest fleet of charter fishing boats were moored. At the top of this picturesque scene a steel frame bridge, there since the early 1900s, sat as a crown.

To the west, the expanse of the lake and the lakefront cottage community where, as a child, I spent my summers.

From here, nestled in ancient poplars, I could see the nineteenth century cottage that my parents owned.

The sun rose out of the watery horizon and sliced through the clouds giving the early morning sky a brilliant orange hue. It was going to be a good day. Gray waves broke over the rocks, and the northwest wind washed over me. If ever there was a place to feel the presence of God, it was on this pier. The constant sweep of the light from the lighthouse gave me a feeling of comfort. In my younger days, this was where I solved all of the major problems of my world. Maybe it was the memories. Maybe it was the starting of a new day. Maybe God was here. I was never sure. Either way, I was home.

It was two months ago that I packed up, and left Fort Lauderdale. My plan was to leave at first light. I wanted to watch the sunrise on the ocean. My last night in Florida, Pete Stiles, Ben McManus, and Matt Seelbinder showed up at my dock with a collection of friends and strangers that they had gathered along the way. Our destination was the Southport Raw Bar. It was their plan to give me a proper send-off, and they would not take 'no' for an answer. The evening was spent eating raw clams and drinking frosted mugs of Heineken. It turned into one of those parties that enveloped the entire bar, as businessmen, college students, sailors and construction workers all joined in shaking my hand and wished me well. Somewhere along the line we picked up a group of teachers from Canada. They were in town for a conference, and with several others that were from Fort Lauderdale, and all out for a night on the town. One woman in the group, apparently arriving alone, had the improbable name of Barbie Shine.

She was a thin thing of indeterminate age; her hair

was blond, and her body fully tanned except where here bikini straps lived. She and I left about midnight when she offered to show me her pool. We sped in her Porsche 911 up Federal Highway to Oakland Park Boulevard, finally turning onto Bayview Drive. On the pool deck, with the south Florida moon providing the only light, we drank gin and tonics in heavy frosted tumblers. The pool was built in the shape of an anchor. The shank of the anchor went under a bank of sliding glass. The ring at the top of the anchor shank was inside the house. If someone wanted to swim into the living room all they had to do was to go under a pair of sliding glass doors and resurface inside.

When our drinks were gone, that's how I got into the house. When I returned from inside the house with two fresh drinks, she was swimming. Her clothes lay in a pile by the edge of the pool. The lights in the pool cast an eerie green tinge onto her tan lines. I set the drinks by the edge of the pool and joined her, my clothes adding to the impromptu pile. We swam, and drank, and made love. First on the deck of the pool. Then after rushing naked into the house, our wet bodies chilled by the central air, in her bed. Where we took the time to explore, to get to know each other, find what worked, what didn't. Finally, as the sun was beginning to break, we slept. The harsh light of the noonday sun revealed that despite the pleasure of the night before I was in a stranger's bedroom looking at a stranger looking at me. This was the first time since my divorce. I was glad when she finally dropped me off at the marina. I kissed her, happy that we had the night, and happy that she was dropping me off, and happy that I was heading out in a few hours. Her eyes told me that she felt the same way. She honked the horn a couple of quick beeps and waved as she spun her wheels out of the parking lot.

I moved to Fort Lauderdale fifteen years ago when I left Saunders Point. Living in Florida, I wrote a couple of books and made a ton of money. Living the good life, I didn't even open the Word program on my laptop for a couple of years. When I finally did, feeling the financial crunch of two years without income, there was nothing there. Not even a bad idea. Creditors called every day. Cindy threw me out; it all came crumbling down. Resigned to fate, I signed the papers that transferred ownership of the house near the beach and finalized the sale of the condo in Key West. All of my bank accounts had been drained, my house, the stocks, and the condo were gone. I signed the papers for the divorce. In the space of an hour at my attorney's office, I became a broke, homeless, single man. Between the bank, the lawyers, and Cindy, now my ex-wife, they had taken everything I owned.

Almost. I kept the boat. I walked out of the lawyer's office, hopped a cab to the marina, and a week later, after sleeping off the party at the Southport, I was cruising out of Lauderdale with the mainsail set, autopilot set north. I was thinking about that last argument. I could still remember how that weekend started.

"I can't do this anymore," she had said as our eyes locked over the kitchen table. "I just can't." She had started in just as soon as I walked in the door. It had been a pretty good day. After breakfast, I drove down to the Sunrise Harbor marina. I was supposed to be cleaning up my 38-foot sailboat, *Bella Cosa,* but I spent most of the day with a fishing pole and a beer in my hand. It was about 4 o'clock, and I just got home. I had been out in the south Florida sun all afternoon. I was baked. I was looking forward to a shower, getting something to eat, and then crashing on the couch. I was not in the mood for what had become our only way of communicating. One single argument that centered mostly on my faults.

"What now," I said, "same old thing?"

"Don't be an asshole, Arn," JerryJack said. JerryJack was Cindy's younger brother. He was a big man, standing about 6'5" and weighed in on the far side of 300 pounds. He was seated next to Cindy at the kitchen table. "Cindy wants you to leave."

I just laughed. "This is my house."

"Not no more," he said and stood up. "It belongs to Cindy now."

"Bullshit."

"And she wants to divorce your sorry ass." He took a step towards me. JerryJack and Cindy grew up west of Fort Lauderdale, in the Everglades. JerryJack worked as a fishing guide, and still lived out there in the house they grew up in. He was a hard drinkin', hard livin', hard fisted redneck who settled most of his problems by punching out whoever got in his way. I did not want to go that way with him.

"JerryJack," Cindy said, "I can do this. You can go now." JerryJack looked disappointed.

"I ain't leavin', Cin," he said as he sat back down, and folded his arms across his chest. They looked like they were bigger than my legs.

"Cindy, is this true? You want a divorce?"

"I just can't do this anymore. I just can't." She started to cry. JerryJack was glaring at me. He looked like he was ready to pounce.

"Cindy..." I said.

"I got a lawyer," she said through the tears." He thinks you should move out today."

"Move out?!" I cried as I slammed my fist into the refrigerator. It jumped back into the wall. Family pictures and magnets crashed to the floor. "What the fuck!"

JerryJack started moving just as I hit the refrigerator. He grabbed me and threw me against the wall that separated the kitchen from the living room. Air burst from my lungs and I struggled to breathe and hold my balance. I was gasping. I dropped to the floor. JerryJack was in a fighting stance; his right fist cocked and ready to finish me off. I sat there trying to decide if I was stupid enough to take him on. I was mad enough for sure. I just sat there.

"JerryJack!" Cindy's voice cracked like a whip. JerryJack stopped in his tracks. He looked like a naughty schoolboy who just got caught by the teacher. "That's enough of that. You go on home now." He looked at her and looked at me wheezing against the wall. He lowered his fists.

"Cindy," he started.

"Just go," she commanded. She spoke quietly. There was no anger in her voice now. "Please?" More tears. He nodded, walked back to the table and set his fishing hat on his big round head. I had never seen him go anywhere without it.

"You ain't seen the last of me," he growled. He kept his eyes on me as he left. He stomped out, and neither of us said anything until the sound of his old truck faded. I started breathing normally and sat down at the table. Cindy sat in the chair in the other side. The pictures and magnets were still on the floor.

"Are you ok?" I just looked at her.

"Cindy," I said, "a lawyer?"

"You know we can't go on like this. Something has to change."

"But I gotta move out? You want me to move out?"

"The lawyer said it is the best way."

"What do you say?"

She hesitated. "I think it's for the best, don't you?"

"Jesus Christ, Cindy, I gotta move out? Where, the fuck, am I supposed to go?" I stood up again. I couldn't just sit there and calmly discuss this.

"Well, "she said with a tiny sarcastic smirk, "there's always Bella."

"Bella?" I was yelling now. "I am supposed to live on that dinky little boat while you live here in luxury? Luxury that I paid for? Is that what I am supposed to do?" I was almost standing on my toes. I could not remember being so angry. Not even in the last few months of fighting with Cindy. I didn't know what to do with so much anger.

"Arn, don't make this any harder than it is." I watched as a small tear rolled down her cheek. My anger just grew. I wanted to punish the refrigerator some more.

"You have no idea how hard this is going to be," I said as I slapped the refrigerator again. Cindy jumped out of the chair, ready to run in the other room. She looked afraid. I was just mad. "I gotta go," I said. I slammed the door on my way out. I squealed my tires as I started down the street. At the stop sign, I slammed my palms into the steering wheel several times and squealed them again as I left our street. That seemed to release some of my anger. I could think again. By the time I reached the marina, I concluded that I if I was going to have to live on that damn boat, I might as well be on the ocean. I had to do something. Go somewhere. Fuck Fort Lauderdale. Fuck JerryJack. Fuck Cindy too, and her lawyer. I decided to sail to the condo in Key West. If I left now, I could be there by morning. I had some food aboard, and a bottle of bourbon. I gassed her up, made sure all onboard electronics were working and took off. I made a cheese sandwich and poured a glass of bourbon. I cruised past Bahia Mar. I raised my glass in salute to the former resident of slip f-18. I waved at the cruise ships. I was lighting a Garcia Vega when I passed the jetties. I was feeling better. I set the sails and input my course into the GPS. It was a beautiful south Florida night, and I settled into the cockpit to watch the sunset over the Keys. My mind was all over the place.

I slept a little in the cockpit on the way down, but nervously woke up every couple of hours to make sure I was still on course. One of those times, underneath a clear moonless starlit night sky, I realized that Cindy was right. Something had to change. But what exactly? I was Arn Maxwell, the writer. And she was my wife. While I didn't go in for the glitz that comes with success, this was who I was. A writer. Sure, times have been hard lately, but we could get through it. I looked at the stars. Couldn't we? Sometimes writers go through dry spells. I had been through dry spells before. I always came through with something. Always with something that made money too. Never this long though. No reason that I wouldn't this time too. I just had to buckle down. I sat in the cockpit, lit a cigar, and stared at the sky. Out on the ocean, with no other light, I could see every star in the sky. I rode, and stared, and smoked. The only noise was the sound of the boat cutting through the waves. I had to do something. Ok, so do something. I would stay in Key West for a few days and let things cool down. When I got back, Cindy and I would work something out. I would start work on my next book. I would write enough to get my agent interested, get an advance from the publisher, and we would dig ourselves out of this hole. Together. Feeling good about my decision, I tossed the rest of my cigar overboard, and went to sleep.

I found a mooring ball right in front of the Truman Annex about 10 am. We had been one of the first people to buy when the condos were built. After making sure that Bella was secure, I taxied my little Saturn into shore. I walked up Southard Street past the Annex. I was headed to the Cuban Coffee Queen for a Keywester, and cup of café con leche. I had discovered Cuban coffee on one of my trips to Miami, and since I found the Queen, I stopped every time I was in Key West. After a second cup, I walked back to the Annex. I unlocked the door to the condo just before noon. The air was stuffy and humid. And a little musty. I thumbed down the thermostat, and soon, the whirring of the new air conditioner was joined by cool clean air. I sat in the living room and let it wash over me. I fell asleep in the chair.

When I awoke, the sun had dropped behind the buildings. It was cold in my house. I went to the thermostat. I had turned it to 65 degrees. I turned it up a little and hopped into the shower. I felt clammy. I was grimy with sweat, and salt from the journey. The cool water felt good. It woke me up. I was feeling better. I decided to walk up to Bagatelles for some hogfish, and a slice of Key Lime Pie. I slipped into a pair of khaki shorts, and a polo shirt with Truman Annex embroidered over the breast pocket. I had picked it up somewhere, and I kept it the condo in case I needed a clean shirt. I had left all my clothes in Fort Lauderdale. I found myself wishing that Cindy was here. She loved Bagatelles. Probably more than me.

I moved to the closet in the kitchen. This had become our junk collection spot. It contained cleaning tools, fishing tackle, old boxes of stuff we didn't use but didn't want to give away, and paint. And in the back, under some boxes, an old toolbox. I put it there right after we moved. There were no tools in it. For years, when the money was flowing free, every time we came here, I would throw whatever was in my wallet into the box. My thinking was that I didn't want to get caught without money. There was more than enough to cover everything else. I didn't miss the bills I left in the box. I dug the box out of the closet and dumped it out onto the dining room table. There was a lot. We had never used any of it. I counted it. Holy shit. About 35 thousand dollars. Man, a hundred here, a couple hundred there. It adds up. Fast.

I just stared at the piles on the table. There was a time that I thought that 35 grand was nothing. Now it was everything. This would surely help out when I got back to Lauderdale. We could use it to hold back some of the creditors while I was writing the book that would save us. Carefully, I repacked the toolbox. I kept a couple of hundred out for my evening and put the box under my bed. I didn't want to forget it. I got a little paranoid and put it back in the closet. I locked the closet.

I slipped my boat shoes on and headed out the door. I walked up Southard to Duval. It was busy. A cruise ship must be in. Carnival it said on most of the t-shirts. I walked up Duval past Sloppy Joes. I thought I should stop for a drink. Later, I guess. The bar was filled with those stupid t-shirts.

"Maybe after supper," I said out loud to no one, and walked past.

Bagatelles was busy. I found a spot at the bar and ordered a Rum Runner. I told them dark rum only. It was excellent. The restaurant was busy all evening, so after a couple Runners, I decided to eat at the bar. The Hogfish was done just right. The Key Lime Pie, perfect. I was glad I decided to come here. I finished my meal and stepped back out into the evening. I lit a cigar and decided on a slow walk up Duval. If it wasn't too busy, I would stop at Sloppy Joes. It felt like a literary pilgrimage every time I was there. Almost like I wasn't a writer if I didn't at least have one drink in Hemmingway's favorite haunt. It was usually more. Maybe tonight, I could absorb some inspiration. I needed an Idea if I was going to pull my life out of the flames.

I walked up the street. Most of the cruise ship people had returned to the boat. The locals were starting to come out. As I walked into the bar, a couple of the more colorful characters walked by. The street was changing right in front of my eyes. I decided that it would be a good idea to make it an early night. I found a seat next to the open doors. My favorite bartender, Becky, was working. I ordered a Manhattan. Fruity drinks were ok, but what I really liked was bourbon. I turned to the stage. Some guy was singing the "Folsom Prison Blues." He was doing a pretty good job. I turned back to my drink. I sat quiet for a while.

"Everything ok over here Arn?" It was Becky. "You look like you lost your best friend. By the way, where is

Cindy?"

"She's back at home," I said. "I came alone." Becky looked at me with her eyebrows raised. "Yeah," I said.

"What happened?" She asked.

I don't know why, but I told her. I guess I needed to tell someone. She had a sympathetic face. I finished up. "So, I came down here to get away, and I came into this bar to see if I could get a little inspiration." I held up my glass. "It worked for Papa."

"How's that workin' for ya," she laughed.

"Not so good. All I am getting is drunk."

"I think that's all it did for him, too." She laughed. "Writin' anything?"

"Well, right there is what seems to be the problem. I can't seem to even come up with a bad idea."

"And this is your solution?" She mixed another drink. She didn't take any money. "You know what they say, don't you?"

"No," I said. "What do they say?"

"The definition of insanity is doing the same thing over and over, expecting a different result." She walked to the other side of the bar. A couple from the cruise ship was leaving. She cashed them out and cleaned up the bar. She didn't come back.

She was right. With no good story ideas, how did I think I was going to make this plan work? There was the money, but that would be gone just as soon as I got home. That meant that I realistically had to have a good story working by next week at the latest. I looked at the picture of Hemingway on the wall behind the stage. "I don't know about you," I said to the picture, "but it doesn't work that way for me." I turned back to the bar. The guy with the guitar ended his set. It was quieter, I could think a little. Maybe I should make a change. Let it all go. Just go back to Lauderdale, give Cindy her divorce, and everything else, find a job, start a new life.

I could just stay here. Why did I have to go back anyway? And do what? I would lose the condo. I would have to find work and a place. Maybe I could go back and find a job. I knew a lot of people in South Florida, something would come up. I took a sip and nodded to Becky. That's what I would do. Go back, throw everything into the pot, except Bella. I could live on Bella pretty cheap. Things would be different, but we could both move on. I don't know if it was the alcohol or the sea air, but I felt really good. Better than in a long time. Like a weight was lifted. I threw a couple of twenties on the table and waved to Becky. Duval Street was hopping. Locals had driven all the tourists inside, and it was a street-long party. I kept my head down as I walked. I didn't want to get drawn into that scene. Having made my decision, I wanted to get home. I wanted to spend one last night in the condo and leave tomorrow morning.

I was up with the sun the next morning. After another Cuban breakfast, I walked down to my skiff. I was a little melancholy. Who knew when I would be back? I was quiet as I motored back out to Bella. I stowed the dingy and its little electric motor. I stashed the old toolbox under my bed. In minutes, I was heading out to sea. I had a cigar in my mouth as I set the sails. I set the GPS and settled into the cockpit behind the wheel. It was going to be good day.

It was early evening when the condos of Fort Lauderdale came into sight. I took the wheel off of auto and looked at the compass. I was heading north. It occurred to me at that moment that I could just keep going north. I always knew that I was connected to Saunders Point by water. But go to New York? It was a dream of mine to make that trip by water. That would certainly be making a change. What the hell would I do up there? Beats me. I guess I could just go and visit Aunt Liz. Maybe stay for the summer, then come back to my new life. Keep the toolbox under the bed. Nobody needed to know about it. Hmmmm. An interesting idea. I would have to give it some more thought. Worn out from the trip, I pulled Bella into the slip, and headed home to talk to Cindy.

The meeting with the lawyers and my last night in Lauderdale were two months later. It was noon when I finally passed the jetties. Spring was just getting started. I thought it would be a good time to get to New York. All the snow would be gone. Confusion, anger, and self-doubt crewed as I sailed up the eastern coast of the United States. Throughout the trip, during the evening and rainy days when my mind wasn't occupied with the business of sailing, I could only think of one thing. That flat rock near Saunders Point.

I arrived at Dale Davis' Golden Sunset Marina under the stars. It had been a long, solitary day aboard Bella. I sailed west from Mud Bay just as the sun was rising. As the sun was setting, Saunders Point came into view. The offshore breeze that I had been riding all day had died. The sails were all stowed, and I was under power when I passed the lighthouse. Forgotten thoughts enveloped me as I motored past the break-wall and between the piers that stood as stone sentinels guarding the harbor. The lighthouse beckoned. 'Welcome home,' it called. Motoring into an empty slip at the end of the dock and securing my boat for the night, I dismissed this unexpected and unwanted wave of sentimentality as just being tired and glad that the journey was done.

'Bella' was by no means the largest boat on the lake, but ever since my marriage ended, I had discovered that she was comfortable enough to be my living quarters. It had been in much better days that I had bought her, on a whim, at an auction in Fort Lauderdale. It had taken a little bit of effort to get her back into shape, but it was worth it. I fell in love with her on the first voyage. Now she was all that I had left. That and about $25,000. 00 that constituted the last of my life savings All that remained from the money I had managed to hide from Cindy, the legal eagles, and the money people. It was now safely stashed in a toolbox under my bunk in the bow. At 38 feet, she was just right for one man to handle. It was on that first voyage after I bought her, that I conceived the idea of coming back home by boat. The knowledge that the water I was in directly connected me to Saunders point, and my past, filled my imagination as I sailed. It wasn't until that weekend in Key West, that I decided that the time was right to get out of town. Life had turned sour in Florida. I needed a change of scenery, a vacation; find the sweetness again. Now here I was. I wasn't sure why.

I hadn't told anyone that I was coming, telling myself that I was shooting for the element of surprise. Truthfully, with the exception of Aunt Liz, there was no one that I really wanted to see anyway. She had raised me since I was ten. My parents were long gone, twenty-five years resting in the Newport Protestant Cemetery. They were victims of a hit and run. The guy was headed home from a graduation party, drunk. They found him passed out in his front yard. He is still in Attica; or so I heard.

The plan was to spend a few weeks at her place on the other side of the lighthouse, then head back to Lauderdale and figure out what I was going to do with my stalled career, and my life. It had been three years since I had written anything worth reading. All I had left was the Bella Cosa, and my stash. That wasn't going to last very long. I was going to have to do something. Soon. The problem was that I didn't quite know what. The idea of a day job was unappealing. I hadn't worked for someone else since the early days in Florida, when I was on the construction crew. I had nothing. It was this fact, and the fact that I was unable to wake the muse, that made me think that now was the time for this trip.

As I stood there in the early morning, with the lighthouse, the lake, my memories, and my thoughts, I felt the presence of God, and maybe that was the muse peeking out from behind the bright orange sunrise. Still unsure, I did feel a little better.

I recalled the day I left Saunders Point. We had a family dinner the night before. Uncle Bud sat at the head of the table. His real name was Bradley, but everybody called him Bud, except for Aunt Liz. He sat back after dinner, and after lighting his ever-present Garcia Vega, spent the rest of the evening finishing off a pitcher of Manhattans and giving me advice. Uncle Bud died suddenly about five years ago, and I did not return for his funeral. I was down off the coast of Haiti, fishing, and by the time that I received word that he passed, the funeral was over, as was the ceremony of scattering his ashes in the lake.

As soon as I heard, I phoned and Aunt Liz said that she understood, but distance didn't diminish the sadness and disappointment I heard in her voice. I felt so bad that I had not talked to her since. As I stood here this particular morning, in this spot, I could see her house, and still felt bad. I had lost everything over the last few years: family, career, and my possessions. Perhaps this upheaval was what drew me back to the end of this old rock pier.

I began the walk back. The day was starting. The west wind grew stronger, and the lake water chilled as waves broke against the rocks covering the pier and me. Wet, and shivering, I walked through the parking lot of the Baited Hook Diner. Overlooking both the harbor and the lake, the Baited Hook was one of those places that could not be built today. The building was too close to the water, and the land was far too valuable for an old greasy spoon. But it was also the kind of place where you could still get two eggs, toast and coffee for a couple of bucks.

When my parents were alive, we used to walk to the 'Hook' for breakfast every Saturday morning in the summer. I ordered a cup of coffee and slid into a booth to dry. The place still looked the same, with its red, vinyl-covered stools at the main bar. The names of people that had eaten there over the years were carved into the dark wood booths that lined the outside walls underneath the oversized windows. The place was about half full. Nobody recognized me, and I did not recognize a single person.

I finished my coffee, threw two dollars on the table, and walked out. There was an old picture of me behind the cashier. It was a picture of me with longer blond hair and clean-shaven, blue eyes shining, without my glasses. The title of my first book, *Outside the Dreams*, was in big letters at the top, and someone had written 'local boy makes good' at the bottom. I pulled my hat down further over my eyes and absentmindedly stroked my beard as I walked out.

I started the five-minute walk back to the Bella Cosa. Oak trees on both sides protected the gravel walkway from the wet wind. The sun rising into a bright blue sky gave promise to a beautiful late spring day. Saunders Point hadn't changed much in the last fifteen years. I walked past the dock where I used to fish with my best friend, past the path that led to the old tennis courts where I had my first kiss. Past the charter boat marina and the Point Breeze Restaurant and Bar, where I had my first job, busing tables. Finally, I passed under the big sign that signaled the entrance to Dale Davis's Golden Sunset Marina. This sign was a huge archway that was painted gold. The top of the arch was a glorious orange-red sunset with a picture of a smiling sailor with one eye, waving. As a kid, I thought this was Popeye's house. As I grew up, I realized that the sailor looked more like old man Davis than the legendary cartoon sailor. I strolled to slip fifteen, at the end of the dock, where the Bella sat patiently waiting. There was a newspaper on the bow, folded tightly, wrapped with a rubber band and with a bright green post-it-note on the top that read "Compliments of the Sunset Marina." I picked up the paper and walked to the end of the pier to check my lines. When I saw that they were secure, I sat on the dock, in a folding chaise by the stern, and looked upriver. I had to admit to myself, there were few places in the world that could compare to the view that was before me. Boats of all shapes and sizes lined up as far as the eye could see. There were orchards on the east side, and in the distance the picturesque old steel bridge that carried Route 18 over the Oak River. This remnant of another time appeared to be out of place, yet right where it should be, nestled in an endless sea of trees. The newspaper went unnoticed as I took this all in. The bridge rested to the south; the lake gleamed to the north. I felt like a fugitive. I had run away from my life; nobody knew where I was. I was free, for the first time in my life. At that moment, I didn't have a responsibility to anyone in the world. If I were to back Bella out of this slip, and sail away, nobody would even know that I had been here. I lit a Garcia, opened the Newport Morning Gazette and smiled. Of all of the places in the world that I had seen over the past few years, when it came time to get away, to disappear, I had run here, to the past. Arn Maxwell had come home.

TWO

I locked up the Bella Cosa and walked up to the marine store at the other end of the dock. Even a fresh coat of paint couldn't totally hide the wear and tear of nearly a century by the water. The store front faced the river, and there was a covered porch with a couple of picnic tables on the side facing the parking lot and road. There wasn't anybody around. Through the aluminum door covered with faded cigarette advertising, I went in. I was immediately accosted by a blast of arctic air as I entered. The store was larger than it looked from the outside. It had a good inventory of boating supplies in one section; hardware in another, tackle, and assorted fishing supplies; and in the other room, a convenience store. 'Milk, Eggs, Beer, Gas,' the faded sign announced over the archway that split the store. Surveillance cameras filmed blind spots, so that the lone clerk could stand behind the cash register and watch a video monitor keeping track of the entire store.

"Can I help you, sir?"

I looked at the clerk and could not help but think that I had seen him before. He was about twenty. His curly hair hung in his eyes, and down his back. I stared at his round face. His nametag only said 'Dale.' "Are you the guy who came in on that Florida boat last night?" He asked.

"Yeah, I got in about dark," I said. "I put into fifteen, I hope that's ok."

He nodded. "Did you really come all the way from Fort Lauderdale?" He must have read the back of the boat. 'Bella Cosa' was painted on the walnut stained stern, in a half circle, in ornate letters. Fort Lauderdale Fla. was gold leafed on the bottom.

"Yeah, I started a couple of months ago."

"That's cool. Someday I want to do something like that. Anything to get out of this boring town." Boy did that sound familiar. "What brings you to our little part of the world? Just passing through?"

"No, I'll be here for a few days. I'm visiting some relatives, and my old hometown."

"Well, the slip fee is 40 a night. And fifteen is good with me, if it's good with you. It works out to about a dollar a foot, I guessed her at 40 feet." He quickly wrote up the paperwork, "That includes the water and electric hookups. If you want phone or cable that will be extra." He looked up when he got to the part about how long I was staying.

"I don't know. Let's say a week to start." I pulled six fifties out of my wallet from the five hundred I had rescued from the shoebox. "No phone, no cable."

Dale carefully finished the paperwork, wrote out a receipt and gave both to me to sign. I placed a twelve pack of Labatt's and the refrigerator magnet that I had in my hand on the counter. It was a smaller version of the picture of old Dale Davis that was on the main entrance, squinty eye and all. It was then I realized why the kid behind the counter looked familiar. He must have been a Davis.

"Do you know where I can get a car to rent?" Another twenty for my groceries. Dale gave me change and put the magnet in a small bag.

"Well, you want a new car, you can call the Chevy dealer up in Newport, or we can let you use Ol' Betsy." He pointed out the window to the parking lot. Ol' Betsy turned out to be a 1970 Dodge Power Wagon. The original paint on the oversized four-wheel drive pick-up had faded long ago to an undistinguishable tan-green color spotted gray where someone had done bodywork to keep it from rusting away. "We use it to plow snow in the winter and to haul boats in the summer. She doesn't look like much, but the engine is just like brand new. I rebuilt it myself. In my spare time I do the bodywork." He said with pride. "We usually get ten bucks a day."

"I'll let you know," I said. There was no way that I was going to be seen in that thing. I was used to driving new cars. My last car, now my ex-wife's car, had been a Volvo. I decided to call the Chevy place. I took my change and paperwork, stuffed it all in my pocket, and walked back outside. There was an old-fashioned phone booth by the corner of the building, complete with a phone book. *Only in Saunders Point*, I thought. I had a perfect view of Ol' Betsy as I found the number for Shelp Chevrolet in Newport. A woman answered. Yes, they could get a car for me. It would only be $49. 99 a day. They would be happy to deliver it as soon as one became available. In about three days. I thanked them very much and went back to close the deal on Ol' Betsy. I didn't want to wait for three days, and as I gave my new friend Dale another two twenties and a ten, I was concerned about my ever-shrinking stash on the Bella Cosa.

The power struggle with Ol' Betsy started as soon as I pulled out of the marina parking lot. The first pothole sent me flying off the hard vinyl seat, hanging on only to the steering wheel and the gearshift knob that looked like an Eight Ball stolen from the local pool hall. With bad shocks, a standard transmission, and no power steering, Ol' Betsy was a little hard to handle. I managed to wrestle her under control just in time to make the right-hand turn onto Wilsonmile Road and my parent's old cottage.

Ol' Betsy rumbled as I sat, parked in the road behind the cottage. The front porches upstairs and downstairs, wrapped around three sides facing the lake, and a screened-in porch faced the road. All intact, looking well kept. It looked just like I remembered it. I sighed as I put the truck in gear and drove on, back up Wilsonmile to Old Oak River Road. I slowed as I reached the intersection where Old Oak River Road met Route 18. This was the old steel bridge that I saw from the dock and was where Route 18 crossed Oak River. This was also the intersection where the drunk driver racing across the bridge had killed my parents. I drove through and headed for Newport. Old Oak River Road connected with New Oak River Road, which was the main road into Newport. I stopped just outside of town. This intersection was known as Five Points as there were five roads that all met at the same place. Ahead of me was the business district of Newport. From here you could also see the bridge that crossed the canal, and in the distance, the steeple of Newport Presbyterian. This nineteenth century church was the tallest structure in town. When the canal was built, Newport was the center of commerce in this part of the state. Once a bustling town, now, one hundred years later it was a 'bedroom community' and just looked old. I drove down the road where my grandparent's farm had been, only to find that the farm and house were gone. Wal-Mart stood where I had played as a kid.

I drove back into town and crossed the Oak River. This side of town was mostly residential. Along the river was the old section. Antique mansions that had been turned into apartments dominated the river's edge. I passed through tree-lined streets, through the new section, and out of town again towards Newport Protestant Cemetery. As old as Newport, it was built on the highest ground in the county. I shuddered as I drove through the sandstone arch and wrought iron gate, past the old chapel, and monuments to the town's founding fathers, to the quiet, shaded spot in the back corner where my parents rested. An urn of fresh mums stood by their stone, and the whole place looked well maintained. Jim and Diane Maxwell. I realized that they had been my age when they died, thirty-five. I cleaned the dried grass cuttings off the bottom of the stone. *Together in eternity*, it said. Aunt Liz had picked that out; she was my mom's older sister. I placed a penny on the stone. I turned and saw where Uncle Bud had been laid; a new stone sat right next to my parents. An urn of fresh mums stood next to that one also. Must be Aunt Liz's doing. Another penny. A small tear escaped and rolled down my cheek as I silently apologized before I got back into the truck.

I stopped at the McDonald's that had been built where my best friend Larry had lived. Driving through, I devoured my double cheeseburger and coffee as I headed back towards the lake, and Aunt Liz's house.

Driving down the east side of the river was a different experience. Once outside the village, I passed into farmland. The fields were alive with farm machinery and workers. Most of them were bent over, and almost all of them were Hispanic. Way back before the canal had come through, this road had been the main road through the area. The intersection at Ridge Road had been the hub of commerce then. A tavern that had been a stopping point for stagecoaches still stood, as the Newport Inn, and was one of the nicest restaurants in the area. Aunt Liz and Uncle Bud brought me to the Newport Inn when my parents died, and then again when I graduated from high school. Across the street was a farm market, and next to that was a schoolhouse and church built back when this area was growing. The school was a museum of local history now. I continued towards the lake. There were orchards on both sides of the road as I headed north. I looked at the sign for Saunders Point Lighthouse as I turned onto Lower Lake Road towards Aunt Liz's house.

The last time that I was on this road, I was in my '86 Chevy Citation, with all of my worldly possessions, driving off towards Florida, and my future. I drove about a half-mile down the road to the point where the road was right next to the lake and stopped. I was only about a half mile away from the house I grew up in, and the woman that raised me: the woman that I hadn't spoken to in five years. I was nervous. Apprehensive, I eased Ol' Betsy back onto the road.

The first thing that hit me as I pulled into the driveway was that the house and grounds looked unkempt and run down. It was always a source of pride for Aunt Liz and Uncle Bud to have everything in perfect order. As a kid, this was always a problem, as I always had chores to do, and I was constantly being scolded for forgetting to remove my shoes whenever I entered the house. There was a dusty black Cadillac in the driveway, but other than that, it appeared that no one was home. I parked Ol' Betsy next to the Caddy. The new-built motor backfired as I shut it down. It sounded like a shotgun.

"Who is it? Who's there?" Aunt Liz stood behind the wooden screen door as I walked up the porch steps. The steps were worn and needed a coat of paint, but the most shocking sight was Aunt Liz herself. She was thinner than I had ever seen her. The black dress she wore hung on her as if bought for a larger person. Always tall and erect, she now hunched over and appeared to be holding onto the side of the door for support.

"Aunt Liz?" I asked as I approached. I was having trouble with the sight that was before me. "Aunt Liz, it's me. It's Arn."

"Arn?" She squinted as she searched for some recognizable feature. She reached for the pair of glasses that hung around her neck. She had never seen me with a beard. No one had. I started growing it when I left Fort Lauderdale. I was looking for anonymity. It had worked. It wasn't until she put the glasses on, and our eyes met, that she knew it was me standing on her porch. Tears filled her eyes as her face softened, and she opened the door and moved into my arms.

"Aunt Liz, stop crying." She seemed so frail. I was afraid to hug her. She was as light as a feather.

"Why didn't you call? Why didn't you tell me that you

were coming?" Through the tears, her eyes were angry, but she was smiling.

"I wanted to surprise you." She stepped back to look at me. She regained her composure. She looked much older than I had remembered. Sure, it had been fifteen years, but she looked much older than the 70 or so years that I knew her to be. It was obviously hard for her to get around. We stood and looked at each other, both drinking in the fact that we were together again.

"Aren't you going to let me in?" I followed her inside. The general feeling of neglect followed us through the door. As I walked into the house that she and Uncle Bud had built together, I could see that entranceway floor was cluttered. Passing the kitchen, I noticed the dirty dishes in the sink. Something was definitely wrong. She started fussing. Closing the door to the kitchen, she hid the newspaper under the sofa pillows.

"We're out front, on the porch. Tom just brought me home from a funeral," she said as she shuffled down the hallway. Liz Coleman was one of the most active, energetic people that I had ever known. Even as a kid, it had been hard to keep up with her. She was always on the move. I couldn't remember a time when she wasn't working on this project or that. Including the house, which was always spotless. This old woman walking before me moved as if she was in pain. When she finally made it to the porch and sat down, the relief was evident in her entire body. I could not hide the concern that was on my face.

"Aunt Liz?" I started to ask what was going on, when I was interrupted.

"Who do we have here, Liz?" I turned and for the first time noticed the tall, handsome man sitting in a chair on the other side of the table.

"It's my nephew, Arn, Reverend Earle."

"Your nephew Arn? Arn Maxwell, the writer?" He stood and offered his hand.

"I used to be," I said as we shook hands. He gave me a look that radiated both understanding and questioning. "How are you, Mr. Earle?"

"I am a huge fan," he sat back down. "Your Aunt is always talking about you. It is good to finally meet you. Please, call me Tom. How I am, is fine," he said, "and running late. Liz, I will leave you to your surprise visitor and get on with my day." He hugged her and shook my hand as he walked towards the door. "I can let myself out." Aunt Liz was silent as the caddy started, and gravel crunched under the tires as Reverend Earle pulled onto the street.

"Where have you been?" Sitting in another one of the wicker chairs, it was easy to forget the frail old woman that I had seen walking through the living room. The old Liz was back. Upright, and erect, anger fired her eyes. Emotion resonated in her voice. "You haven't even called me in five years. FIVE YEARS!" The tears ran again. I turned red with shame. I hung my head. "I have missed you!"

"Aunt Liz, I am so sorry." It was all I could say.

"Sorry doesn't cut it. All this time. Without a word. I had to read about your problems in the newspaper of all places." I could almost see the anger flow out of her. A single tear fell down her cheek. That little outburst, and the effect of my surprise visit, had taken their toll. There, again, was that old lady that I had first seen on the porch. "What are you doing here?"

"I came to visit you."

"Bullshit," She always could see right through me.

"I did too. I needed a change of scenery, everything came to a head, and I don't know why, but I ended up back here on Saunders Point."

"Of course, you came home. You came back to your roots." She looked me in the eye. "You lost everything?" she asked. I nodded. "Cindy too?" I nodded again. She shook her head. After about a minute, she spoke. "Well, where else would you go when you're in trouble?" She looked at me with one eyebrow raised. "I don't mind saying that if you had never left..." She was never one to hold back what she thought, and immediately I felt like I was twelve again.

THREE

After the initial surprise, the excited hugs, and the 'where the hell you been' speech, which was followed closely by my apologies, I was able to take a good look around. The house that Uncle Bud had built, with my father's help, showed signs of neglect, and so did she. The porch needed painting, the lake stone floor in the entryway was covered with mud, and that white semi-patterned residue left by tracking in snow and ice. I remember as a kid trekking to the beach with my Uncle Bud, my father, my little red wagon, and a whole pile of friends. It was our job to find the stones that were used for this entranceway. I knew that at least one had my name written in marker on the bottom. I struggled to remember which one. Aunt Liz didn't look much better; the once proud, beautiful woman looked like the rest of the house. Her once robust figure was gone, and her dress appeared to be two or three sizes too big for her, hanging on her frame like a boat tarp. She had aged. A lot. Something was definitely wrong.

We were sitting on her large screened-in front porch, overlooking the lake and the piers at the entrance to the Oak River. The porch was about fifteen feet wide and ran the full length of the house. Its roof served as a second story sundeck accessed from Aunt Liz's bedroom. Over cut-glass tumblers of homemade iced tea with just the right amount of fresh lemon we began to play the game of what's new. Now after a long afternoon of give and take I had told her my whole story.

"Aunt Liz, are you ok?" We had finished talking about me, and I had finally gotten her to admit that there was something wrong.

"I'm fine," as tears ran down her cheek. "It is just one of those days, with the funeral and all. Cathy was a friend of mine."

"Who?"

"Cathy Paine. I don't know if you would remember her. She lives, lived, on the other side of Newport, on a big farm with her sister, Libby." I did remember them. When we were teenagers, someone started the rumor that they were lesbians and we would drive by their house all the time because none of us had ever seen a real live lesbian. It was Uncle Bud that told me they were really sisters, and that we should quit bugging them. Apparently, the Paine sisters had noticed my car going by their house a little too often. "I don't know what Libby will do now."

Ok, so a funeral excused the mood of the day, but there was more going on. Relentlessly, I stuck a crowbar into the situation and pried until she opened up. She shocked me by stating, finally, that she was almost broke. I always figured that Uncle Bud had left her well off. With the insurance, the house all paid for, and some cash, it should have been more than enough to sustain her for the rest of her life. Now she was telling me it was almost all gone. She floored me again by saying that she had given most of it to Reverend Earle. Furthermore, she was beginning to think that maybe he wasn't on the up and up. I noticed also that after the initial surprise, and happiness of our reunion, she hadn't smiled all afternoon. Comments about the lake, the sunny day and the fleet of recreational sailors silently passing with their multi-colored spinnakers filled by the northeastern breeze, had brought only the mildest of comments. This tired-looking, unkempt old woman was not the same Aunt Liz that had made me toe the line when I was a kid.

"He told me that it was the very best way that I could help." She said by way of explanation.

Aunt Liz sat in a white wicker chair. She looked out over the water as she spoke, avoiding my pointed stare. I was dumbfounded to silence.

"How much did you give him?" I asked. I faced her across the ancient white wicker table.

"Almost one hundred thousand," she looked down at the floor. I choked on my tea. "I'm supposed to give him five more this coming Friday. I am not so sure that I should give it to him. I don't have much left." Tears popped into her eyes as she saw the shocked expression on my face. "Silly, silly, stupid old woman," she barked and ran into the house. I heard a door slam. I sat alone looking out over the lake. The multicolored armada of weekend pirates had passed and now were only tiny colored specs on the horizon.

As I sat waiting for Aunt Liz to return, I turned my thoughts to Reverend Thomas Earle. I had not paid very much attention at the time. Now I was trying to remember every detail. The well-dressed man was graying around the edges of his jet-black hair and had a salt and pepper mustache. His crisp white shirt was spotless. His red tie complemented his dark blue suit perfectly. There was a small white dove pinned to his lapel, a bible in his hands. It looked well used. His tiny, round wire-rim glasses gave him an intellectual look. He had been sitting on a white wicker chair that was part of the porch set I bought for Aunt Liz and Uncle Bud when my first book sold. He carried himself with the confidence of a man who knew who and where he was. I surprised myself with the amount of detail I remembered from that brief encounter. I took a sip of the tea.

"What does he want it for?" She had returned with a bunch of papers in her hands. Her eyes were puffy and red.

"He said that he was supporting a special mission in Africa. We were going to help a school for war-orphaned children. He even has a brochure." She handed me the brochure. "Oxbrown Private School." It had a lot of gold lettering in a fancy script, and a picture of a young emaciated African girl in a private school uniform, holding an armful of books, smiling. She was standing on a tree-lined sidewalk in front of old-looking school buildings. "He said that he was asking all of the members of our congregation to help."

"So, who else has given him money?" I was looking through the brochure. There were lots of pictures of the same girl that was on the cover, and a couple of a boy, and a couple of fancy buildings with students milling around them. I could not find an address, or phone number anywhere. Just a website: www.oxbrown.com.

"I think the Lardner's gave, and Mrs. Grange, she is older than dirt and has more money than God. I wonder how much she gave. Peggy and Stuart Rumson, and Ralph Treats. Those are the ones that I know of. Oh, and Betty Clinton, she told me the other day that she had given him quite a bit also." I did the math, five others at least. If they gave even half of what Aunt Liz gave, that was a pretty good haul for that little school.

"What makes you think that you are being cheated?" I struck a wooden kitchen match and touched it to a Garcia. The pungent smoke enveloped Aunt Liz and she started coughing. "I'm sorry," I said. Looking for an ashtray to put it out, I blew the smoke in the other direction.

"Oh. Dear, that's ok. I just am not used to it anymore. Not since your uncle died," her voice cracked. "He used to smoke those nasty things all the time."

"I know; he is the one that got me started. So, Oxbrown?"

"I miss that smell." She was wistful. She looked out over the lake for a minute. Another small tear. "Well, I don't know if this means anything, but Ralph Treats' daughter Trish, she married the investment banker you know." I didn't know but I nodded. "Well they, Trish and her husband, Richard I think his name is, Dick, or Rick maybe, anyway, they were looking for a private school on account of they have a lot of money and they want the best for their kids. Ralph must have said something about Oxbrown, and Trish got curious one day when she was searching the internet. She could not find any Oxbrown. Nowhere. No how. She called Ralph, and now we are all wondering. Doesn't mean that it doesn't exist." She looked down at the smiling girl. "I want to believe that it does."

"Maybe it does. Tell me about Reverend Earle."

"Well, I don't know. He calls himself T. Whitman Earle. Tom. That is, Thomas is his first name. That's what most of us call him around the church. Tom. Widower, about 60. He came, I guess about five years ago. Yes, that's right. Right after Bud died. Reverend Hamilton did the funeral and left about a month later. Tom, Reverend Earle, spent a lot of time here with me over the next few months. We talked a lot and prayed; he was a great comfort."

"Where did he come from?"

"Jim Lardner. He was on the search committee, he said that he came from Ohio. Some church in Urbana, I think. He was trained in California someplace. I can't remember the name of the school. I could ask Jim. We had to get special permission from the Presbytery to hire him on account of the fact that he is not an ordained Presbyterian minister. Oh, he's ordained, but by another church. Baptist, I think."

"Why did you hire a guy that is not part of your church?" She frowned when I said her church. I had been baptized and raised in that church. I hadn't set foot in any church since I left Saunders Point the first time, about fifteen years ago.

"Well, he applied for the job, and when he came to town, he gave the greatest sermon that any of us had ever heard. Arn, that guy has the Gift with the spoken word. He also had all these great ideas about how to make our church grow and become prosperous again. We have kinda' fallen on hard times." She went into house and returned with a fresh pitcher of lemonade and a clean ashtray for my cigar.

"Has he followed up with any of those great ideas?" I

leaned forward and flicked the long gray ash off the end of my cigar.

"Funny thing is, he did. We have more members, more money. We have become a kind of town center for all humanitarian activity."

"Aunt Liz..." She looked like she was going to cry again.

"Oh, Arn. What am I going to do? The only thing I have left is this house, and now that I don't have any money, they will take that too." She put her head in her hands. I could hear her sniffle. I put my cigar in the ashtray and walked around to where she was sitting. She stood up and as I hugged her, she let go: huge moaning sobs, shakes, shivers. I held her tighter, feeling her frailty and the wetness of her tears soak through my shirt. I was afraid that I would snap her in half if I hugged too hard. At 6'2", 250 pounds, I completely enveloped her. There is a moment in every one's life where the relationship between the child and the parent begins to change. It is a bittersweet feeling, that moment when both begin to realize the child is now a grownup able to handle the role of the parent, and that the deteriorating effects of age are taking their toll on the parent endlessly speeding their way to the day when they become the child.

As we stood there, I started thinking that the good reverend, T. Whitman Earle, Tom I think she said his name was, and I should probably have a chat. I had not been to church in many years and had a real problem with organized worship. In my opinion, God is everywhere, and morality is a personal choice, not a group decision. Some folks, however, Aunt Liz for example, believed differently and worked hard to support these outdated institutions. This guy Earle had played on that belief and cleaned her out. Maybe cleaned them all out. Was he for real? Was the school? I didn't know enough to get a handle on that one. I needed to find someone who could give me the answers I needed. I thought I knew just who to call.

I couldn't help but wonder how many others he had taken. I did the math. One old widow was good for a hundred grand. Say that she was on the high end. Ok, so take a conservative average of 25 thousand apiece. He only needed five or ten of those to build a nice little nest egg. Change locations every couple of years, find new pigeons, live cheap, take their life savings and move on. I stopped myself right there. My imagination was getting the better of me. I was letting my fictional mind take over and create the scenario that I wanted. The one that made sense. But I didn't have any proof. Maybe I was wrong; maybe there really was a school. Maybe he was on the level. I just didn't know enough about it. I had more questions than answers. I decided to do a little checking. See if I could find the truth. Tomorrow I would go and visit the good Reverend T. Whitman Earle.

Aunt Liz insisted that I stay for dinner. She looked like the afternoon had taken its toll. I offered to take her down to the river for dinner at The Northern Point Inn. Once a stop for weary sailors moving trade around Lake Ontario, it had evolved into a bar that served the best chicken wings on this side of the lake. It was located right where the river met the lake, right across the street from the Saunders Point lighthouse. I left the big truck where it stood after Aunt Liz refused to ride in it and we took her ten-year-old Olds. We sat in a booth on the far side of the bar. The large picture windows overlooked the boat launch and the piers. We could not see the sun as it settled into the lake but watched as the evening sky turned rose pink. She barely finished her Zweigle's white hot and was silent as I ripped through a plate of hot wings, huffing and puffing from the sharp burn of the wing sauce. I smiled as sweat broke out on my forehead. I drank draft Labatt beer as fast as I could to put out the fire on my tongue. It wasn't working. This was one thing that I missed by being away from Saunders Point. We finished dinner and after paying, I suggested that we walk out on the pier to watch the end of the sunset. Aunt Liz asked for a rain check. She was worn from the afternoon's confessions, and the unexpected night out, so I took her home. Ol' Betsy and I headed back to the marina. I stepped back aboard the Bella about 8:30. The spring evening had turned cold with the setting of the sun. After buttoning up the boat and turning on the little ceramic heater that I had bought in North Carolina, I turned on my laptop and opened my address book. John Brantford Good, pastor, Eliot Presbyterian Church of Lowell, Mass. We went to the Newport church together. I also graduated from high school with him. We used to call him Johnny B. We used to drink gin and smoke cigars before the youth group meetings. I was shocked when he went into the ministry. I hadn't talked to him in a couple of years. It would be good to hear his voice. I grabbed my cell phone and a cold Labatt from the fridge. I dialed the number that I had written down and got a recording. It was the church office. Closed until tomorrow morning. I didn't have a home number. I dug out my heavy green cable knit sweater and took the beer outside. I lit another cigar. I wrapped myself in a large blanket to ward off the spring chill and sat in my folding flea market chaise on the deck looking over the quiet river, shining in the moonlight.

Spring on Lake Ontario. There weren't many boats in the water, it was still too chilly for the fair-weather crowd. A girl squealed in the marina across the river, and a man laughed. I could hear the sound of traffic on Route 18, and a dog barked somewhere behind me. I sat in silence, took small sips out of the brown bottle and deep drags from the cigar and decided that all of it could wait until tomorrow. I closed my eyes just for a moment.

FOUR

I awoke just as the sun was rising over the orchard on the other side of the river. The damp morning air went deep into my bones, and I shivered as I stood up from the chaise. The muscles in my neck protested as I stretched. Feeling about 90, I stumbled into the galley and started the coffee pot brewing. I decided to shake out the stiffness by going for a run and changed into a pair of black running shorts and a white t-shirt. It had been a couple of months since the last time I ran any serious distance, and I knew it was going to be rough. I made my way carefully out of the bathroom, past the galley and up the stairs to the rear cockpit. At 6'2", I have to duck as I go up the stairs. I am tall enough that sometimes it is difficult to get around my boat without smacking my head. I also have one of those bodies that no matter what I do, I look flabby. I try to run whenever I can, and even holding at about 250, I am proud of the fact that at any time I can usually pull off two or three miles without much effort. I walked slowly through the parking lot. I leaned against the old Dodge. Muscles and tendons creaking and popping, I stretched. I had not run since I left Florida. This one was going to hurt. I thought about my route. If I ran down Wilsonmile Road, along the lake where my parents summer home had been, through the woods, down an orchard lane, to Route 18 and back it would be about three miles, at least that's how I remembered it. The thing that I like most about running is that I can kill two birds with the same stone. While getting the necessary exercise to keep me from completely turning to jelly, I can usually wander around inside my mind, sorting and organizing loose information into reasonable ideas. As I ran out of the marina parking lot, past the old pickup, and down the road, I found my stride. I turned my attention to Aunt Liz. Except for a few thousand, her money was gone. Even if she was careful, she could only survive in that house for a few months. I had some money stashed under the front bunk, but it was not enough to buy her more than a couple more months. And, that would shorten my own viability exponentially. As I lumbered down the lakefront road, I reasoned that the solution was clear. She had to find some way of paying her bills, and if I was going to help her, I either had to begin writing again, or I was going to have to find a real job. Neither prospect seemed promising. I ran past the old cottage. I guess that she could sell, or borrow against the house, but Uncle Bud was so proud when they paid off the first mortgage. Maybe she could move into Newport. She would be closer to everything. I know she wouldn't do that. That was their home. He had worked overtime for years and paid it off three years early. They had owned it free and clear ever since. As I hit the woods, I knew that Aunt Liz would reject this idea. I ran on. As I turned onto Route 18 and the last leg of my run, the effects of the two-month layoff started to show. I was breathing hard and slowing. My rhythm was off. My thoughts were on T. Whitman Earle, and the First Presbyterian Church of Newport. Even if this school in Africa was legit, he took almost all of an old lady's life savings. Not only one, but he had hit several others also. I wondered if he had taken them for all they had also. I decided to ask Aunt Liz. If his actions weren't criminal, they were, at the very least, ethically questionable. Maybe he was a good man, and just blinded by his zeal for his pet project. Maybe he was so charismatic that people were just falling over themselves to give him money. Maybe he was a dirty rotten lowdown conman, defrauding old people and giving clergy all over the world a bad name. With this thought, I was in sight of the marina. I slowed to a walk as I entered the parking lot again. I walked around the old truck, breathing harder than I would have liked, stopping from time to time to stretch my leg muscles on the large chrome front bumper of the old Dodge. Time for a shower, and some breakfast.

Hair still wet, and the first cup of coffee a memory, I stood in the galley, clean pants and a fresh red sweatshirt with the words "yes I did" on the front, scrambling up some eggs; I cut up some sharp cheddar cheese and folded it all together. I slid them onto a plate and took it out to the folding table in the cockpit. I ran back in, grabbed my phone, my laptop and another cup of coffee. The day was beginning to warm up. The sun was bright on my table. I opened the laptop and read the news as I ate. I read an email from my editor, Vern Traffel, wondering if I might want to call him with my latest book, all completed and ready for him to read. Since I had no such book, and didn't see one in the near future, I closed the email without response. It was nine am when I decided to give John a call.

"Eliot Presbyterian, this is Sherry, how are you this morning?" She had answered after five rings.

"May I speak to Reverend Good please?"

"Reverend Good is no longer here, I can transfer you to Reverend Archbuckle."

"No thanks, what I am doing is looking for John Good."

"I'm sorry, sir. Reverend Good hasn't been here for almost two years now." Had it really been two years since we had talked? Another case of the guilts. I had done a good job shutting out my past.

"Can you tell me where he is? I am an old friend."

"I think he wound up in New York somewhere, let me put you on hold, and I'll check." I took my breakfast dishes to the galley and started washing them. I was almost done when she came back on the line.

"Sir, What I had to do is to check with one of the older members of the congregation. She said that he was at the Presbyterian Church in Lockport, New York. I guess they keep in touch. I can give you the number." I wrote down the number.

I got a man's voice when I called the Lockport church. He said that he was just filling in and was going to try to transfer my call. He was adamant that I don't get mad if he hangs up on me. I promised that I would not hold it against him. I was just lighting up a Garcia when the connection was made.

"Arn? Arn Maxwell? Let me think, I used to know an Arnie Maxwell, but that was a long time ago. I think he died. Yeah, He must've died, because I haven't heard from him in years." Sarcasm. In the old days, this was Johnny's biggest gun. If he didn't want you to, you could never get a straight answer out of him. He hadn't changed.

"You know, I would have thought that a man of the cloth would have had to take an oath not to be such a smart ass. Do they still call you Johnny B.?"

"With jerk friends like you, you would be surprised how easy it is to slip back into old habits. How the heck are you? Oh, and nobody calls me Johnny B. anymore." We spent about twenty minutes catching up. I hadn't written anything in three years. He had moved and had two more kids. Three, he was up to now.

"So, to what is it that I owe this great honor?" he asked.

"I want to ask you about a fellow member of the clergy." I gave him the one-minute version of Aunt Liz's situation. "I told her I would look into it. I thought that you might be able to give me some info before I went to see him."

"What's this guy's name?"

"Thomas Earle. He calls himself T. Whitman Earle." I heard scratching as John wrote the name down. I gave him the rest of the details from Aunt Liz.

"You're joking right? T. Whitman? Really? I've never heard of him. Listen, give me about fifteen minutes to make a couple of calls and I will get back to you, ok?"

I sat back for a minute. I took the laptop below and shoved the cell phone into my pocket. I closed the hatches and started hosing Bella down. The air was cold, and the water colder, but she was still a little dingy from the trip up from Florida. There were a couple of salt stains that I could not make go away. I was scrubbing at the one on the bow when the phone rang. It was almost an hour later.

"Johnny B. is that you?" There was silence on the other end of the line.

"Yeah, Arnold." Alright, he had made his point. I never liked the name Arnold. I was called Arnie all through my childhood and had finally managed to get it shortened to Arn when I started writing. I could handle Arn.

"You know, the years haven't made you any kinder," I said. We both laughed. It felt good to talk to him. Even though we hadn't spoken in a couple of years, we picked up where we left off and two years turned into a day. "Did you find out anything?"

"First thing I did was call the Presbytery office. They have records on all past and current pastors that have served in the Presbytery. I know a lady over there, and we sort of do favors for each other. She checked for me. Nothing. You guys are in the Presbytery next door. I called them too, but all they would tell me was that he is the pastor of the church out there. Another dead-end. So, I called my buddy, the pastor over at first Baptist. We play golf together. I remembered that you had said that Liz thought that he was a Baptist. He called the Urbana church, and their minister, I guess he's been there forever, had never heard of him. So, he is not from there. So Reverend Pauly, that's my Baptist friend, Pauly Roman, called a couple of friends and finally found someone who had heard of him. He wasn't in Urbana; he was in Marion. Anyway, According to Pauly's friend, he just up and left one day. No notice, no nothing. It almost wrecked that church, him leaving like that. Pauly's friend said that there were rumors that many of the older parishioners were talking foul play, but nothing ever came of it. Sounds familiar doesn't it?"

"Yeah, if it walks like a duck."

"And talks like a duck."

"That's right old friend. I definitely want to talk to this guy now."

"Yeah, look, I gotta go. Old Man Fender is in the office, he has more money than the whole town of Newport, and I need a new laptop. Don't make it two years before you call again, ok?"

"Yeah, don't move without tellin' me." I started to hang up. "Hey, is Hunky still the Chief in Newport?" Hunky McCabe had been the police chief in Newport when we were sowing our oats.

"You kidding? He's got to be about ninety by now. He retired years ago. I'm not sure. He might be in St. Joe's cemetery. You remember Jack Munger?"

"Yeah." When Hunky wasn't chasing John and me, he was chasing Jack. Jack was a real hard case. I heard he did some time.

"Well Jack is the Chief now."

"Jack is a cop?" I registered my disbelief.

"Yeah, go figure."

"He's a cop and you're a minister. What is this world coming to?" I hung up as Reverend Johnny B. was doing his best to imitate Hank Williams Jr. Something about all my rowdy friends.

FIVE

I refilled my coffee cup, stuffed my laptop and cell phone into my black canvas High Sierra bag, locked up Bella and headed out to Ol' Betsy. I shivered as I hit the cold vinyl seats and turned up the heat. Like a faithful old carthorse that knew where to go, but was in no hurry to get there, she rumbled up the roads that we followed just yesterday heading towards town. As I stopped at the intersection just north of town, I saw the steeple of the Presbyterian Church. I remember as a kid playing the game of trying to be the first one to spot it whenever we came to town. I almost always beat Aunt Liz, but I could never beat Uncle Bud. I continued into town. I parked in the street across from the church. The rebuilt engine popped and sputtered, dying as I hopped out. As I stood and looked at the Gothic sandstone structure in front of me, memories flooded my mind. I leaned against the truck and let them wash over me. Sunday school days, kissing Amy Rogers in the choir loft, and teenage youth group sleep-ins that always led to me and Johnny B. sneaking out in the middle of the night for the bottle of gin and cigars that we had hidden behind the garage. We used to sit behind that garage for hours when everyone else was asleep.

I remembered my parents' funeral, and the crowd of people so great that they had to open the balcony. I sat in front with Aunt Liz and Uncle Bud and got to ride in the front seat of the first limo to the cemetery. I surprised myself that the first memory that I had of that event in over twenty years was of old Hunky McCabe on a police motorcycle leading the procession. I decided to look him up before I went back to Florida. I closed the door of the truck and walked across the street to the church office entrance. The air was damp and stale in the basement office, and I immediately identified the damp smell with the way that Sunday school smelled. The Sunday school rooms were right down the hall.

"Can I help you sir?" A young blond woman moved from behind the secretary's desk to where I was standing in the hall. She was probably thirty; she looked nineteen. She was all business. "Good morning sir, my name is Wendy. I'm the church secretary." She was looking at me as if she could not figure out why I was here. She looked at the shorts and the sandals and made a decision. She held out the notebook in her hand. "If you will just sign your name, I can get the key to the food cupboard. I'm sorry but you can only have one bag."

"I don't need any food; I am looking for Reverend Earle."

"You don't want food? You don't look like a salesman."

"I'm not," the light went on; I realized that she had mistaken me for a homeless man looking for a handout. "I would like to speak to Mr. Earle," I repeated.

"DOCTOR Earle is not in this morning. Today is his day off." She had taken that protective stance that good assistants everywhere take when a stranger is looking to talk to their boss without having the good sense to clear it with them first.

"I need to talk to him about a personal matter. When will he be in?"

"He will be here tomorrow morning, but he has a full schedule." She walked back into the office. "Can I get your name, and tell him what this is about?" She flipped open the calendar on the desk and grabbed a very sharp pencil. I liked this girl. She was efficient and would not commit to anything without more information. "I might be able to get you in if I know."

"Tell him Arn Maxwell wants a few minutes, when it is convenient." I waited for the recognition to kick in. That usually got me in. I really didn't like that part, but always got upset when it didn't happen. She didn't flinch. Three years without a book, and I could not even get recognized in my own hometown.

"If you can get here at nine, he has some time." I agreed and left as she picked up the ringing phone.

"First Presbyterian..." she started in her very young professional voice. I left. I stood outside the building contemplating my next move. I pulled a cigar out of my shirt pocket. The police station was right down the street; I decided to look up Jack Munger. I had no reason to think that I needed to involve the police, but I hadn't seen him in a long time, and maybe he could help me track down something about Earle. DOCTOR Earle. Without lighting the cigar, I started down the street.

I walked into the police station. I was standing in a small room with a window that looked into the offices of the police. The sliding glass window looked as if it was about an inch thick. I pushed the small doorbell button on the left side of the window and from somewhere behind the glass Westminster chimes rang. A young thin cop, looking like Barney Fife in eighth grade walked up and looked out the window. His police uniform was immaculate. Pressed where it should be pressed, shined where it should be shined, the immaculate hardware on his belt looked as heavy as this kid. Dickenson it said on the little tag pinned to his uniform. His dark hair was cut in a classic military crew. His right arm rested on his holstered gun. Pretty heavy security for a small-town operation; either that or I really did look like a homeless man.

'Barney' just pointed to the button and stared. It was that stare that changed my opinion about this guy. On the surface he might have looked like the eighth grade version of Sheriff Taylor's comic sidekick, but the expression on his face was as old as time. I was guilty. Clearly, I had committed some heinous crime and had stopped by to confess. I readjusted my estimate of his age to be somewhere in his thirties. His look tried and convicted me. The solemn face and constantly moving eyes had seen every type of individual through that glass, and most, if not all were guilty. I pushed the button.

"Is Jack Munger around?" His suspicion did not ease.

"Who wants to know?" His voice came across the electronic device deeper than I expected.

"Tell him Arn Maxwell. I am an old high school buddy." Again, I waited for recognition. Nothing. I decided this guy wasn't a reader. His facial expression did not change.

"CHIEF Munger is a very busy man, do you have an appointment?"

"No, I am in town for a few days and I thought I would say hi." I smiled my most photogenic smile. It didn't work. My ex-wife used to tell me not to smile; she said that it looked like I was snarling. Barney must have thought the same thing, as he stepped back towards the radio. He never took his eyes off me.

"Base to unit one. Base to unit number one." He spoke clearly into the microphone on the desk.

"What is it Danny?" Must be Barney's real name. "I told you not to bother me unless it was important. I am with the goddamn mayor." There was not a hint of friendliness in that transmission. Danny went back to looking like that eighth grader; only this time he was the guilty one.

"I'm sorry, chief. There's a guy here to see you." He looked at me hoping for sympathy. I nodded.

"Jesus Christ, Danny. Who the hell is it?" He broke the transmission, and then added, "this better goddamn well be good, or you're going to be working midnights for the rest of your goddamn miserable life." Dickenson looked at me. He had gone back to the cop face. I was a problem. Because of me, the boss was pissed off at him. I shot him my snarling smile again.

"Says his name is Maxwell. Arn?" He looked at me. I nodded. "Yeah, Arn Maxwell."

"Did you say Maxwell?" Dickenson affirmed. "Is he a big fat, tall, ugly lookin' guy? With a face that would stop your mother?" Dickenson looked at me and chuckled.

"Sounds right, chief." Something has passed between

them. Some hidden communication that signaled to the cop in front of me not only was he not in trouble anymore, but that I was not to be suspected. Quite the opposite: I was a friend of the chief and should be respected. For the first time his features softened, and he smiled.

"What the hell does he want, Danny? Jesus Christ, I'm holdin' up the mayor here."

"Chief, Mr. Maxwell says he is in town for a few days and just wanted to say hi."

Well Danny, why don't you go ahead and ask Mr. Maxwell if he can meet me at the Towner in about an hour."

I nodded yes, and Dickenson transmitted that to Jack. He responded by telling him that unless goddamn Osama Bin Laden himself was riding into town, he better not hear from him again until he got back into the office. I left.

SIX

I had an hour to kill. I walked up to the truck and looked around. I was standing in the center of Newport. The historic county courthouse sat in the middle of the square and was surrounded by equally historic churches. The Presbyterian was probably the biggest but did not stand alone in its architectural beauty and significance to the history of the village. Across the street was the Newport free library. Set in the former mansion of one of the village founders, for a hundred years it was one of the cornerstones of the downtown district. I reached into the truck and grabbed my bag. I headed towards the library. They might have internet access there. I had some time; I decided to check out this Oxbrown School.

I entered the dark, cool wooden interior of the library. It was exactly the way that I remembered it. It even smelled the same. Straight ahead was a red-carpeted stairway leading to the second floor. The stairway walls were covered with hand-painted depictions of local history. Through the door on the right was the main room of the library. To the left was an open door with the word 'reference' written on the sign above. I went left. I took a seat at a table in the back of the small room. I was behind a row of bookshelves and alone. I opened my laptop. As I waited for the computer to boot up, I stared out the window at the street. A very large woman hopped out of a brown SUV with a bag of books and three small children in tow. I watched them walk toward the entrance of the library. I did a quick check of my email. Only one message; it was from my ex-wife. "Where the hell are you?" was written in the subject line. I deleted it unopened. I googled Oxbrown private academy- no results; Oxbrown School- still nothing on Oxbrown. Just Oxbrown – a color yes, but no school. I wished that I had kept the pamphlet that Aunt Liz had shown me. I tried '.com,' '.org,' '.edu,' nothing. I would have to ask her if I could see it again. There was a website on the back, but I couldn't remember it. I tried to picture the back of the pamphlet and slapped the table in frustration. Sound echoed through the room louder than I expected.

"Excuse me sir, is everything alright?" I turned to look at the female voice behind me. Dressed in a tan cardigan sweater and a dark brown tweed knee-length skirt, she fit perfectly the stereotype of a librarian. The light brown hair was twirled into a tight bun that sat on the top of her head and only added to the image. She smiled. Her nametag said Kim. I put her at about twenty-five. I wondered if there was a course in Library College that taught prospective librarians the proper technique for a tight hair bun.

"I'm ok." She had startled me. I jumped up.

"You're sure?"

"Yeah, just frustrated that's all."

"Can I help?" She smiled. What a pretty smile. For the first time I noticed her pale blue eyes. The color of the ocean. Just off the beaches of Key West.

"Uh..." I stuttered. I had lost my train of thought. Real smooth, Arn. I struggled to regain my composure. "No, I guess not."

"What are you looking for?" She was looking at the search page on my screen.

"I am trying to find a private school."

"Oh. For your kids?"

"What? No. That is, I don't have any kids."

She smiled. "Teacher?"

"No. I'm a writer doing some research." I decided not to tell her Aunt Liz's business. Small towns are notorious for their informal news channels and I didn't want her name being the lead story on tonight's gossip chain.

"A writer, huh? Ever write anything I might have read?"

"Yeah, I wrote a couple," I hesitated. "Ever hear of a book called *Outside the Dreams*?"

"Yeah, I read it. It was written by a local guy. He wrote a couple more, but *Dreams* was his best. He hasn't done anything in a few years. I think I read that he went bankrupt or something..."

I could actually hear the click, and see the light illuminate the bright blue eyes. A dark shade of red crept out of the sweater and across her face. "Oh my god, you're him."

I smiled.

"Mr. Maxwell, I am so sorry. I didn't recognize you."

"It's ok."

"We have your whole collection here," she said. "It is in a room all by itself upstairs. Evie made a display. She is your biggest fan. She gets so excited by that stuff. She's got your picture and everything. She is going to be so upset. She went home to get a book. She never does that." Three books and a picture. That must be quite a shrine. I decided that it must be a small room. "Wanna go see?" Her smile lit up her whole face. Despite the way that she was dressed, she really was a beautiful girl.

"No thanks." The last thing I needed was a reminder of the past. "Some other time."

"Oh, ok." She looked disappointed.

"Maybe you could help me, though." That smile exploded back onto her face. I explained that I was looking to research a school in Africa, and that I had heard about this one from my aunt, but I could not find it on the internet. She said that there was a listing of private schools in the research library, and that she would go and find it. When she returned, she said that she couldn't find it. She thought that it was probably in storage and retrieving it might take some time. I could wait, but it would be better to stop back tomorrow, she should have something by then. I agreed. She smiled and said something about Evie being jealous, while I packed up my stuff.

"See you tomorrow," she called. I walked out of the library, and as I stood at the intersection waiting for the light to change, I pictured her smile. I realized that I could not wait until tomorrow.

SEVEN

Ol' Betsy shuddered as I bounced through the potholes on the entrance of the Towner's parking lot. The Towner was a small diner in the middle of town. It was clean and always full of customers and pretty young waitresses. A large man in a police uniform stood in front of the restaurant next to a black and white Ford police cruiser; he was talking on his cell phone. He tossed a cigarette butt onto the parking lot as I pulled into the empty spot in front of him. I walked towards him.

"Jesus Christ, Maxwell. I should give you a ticket for littering up my town with that piece of shit." He wasn't smiling. I looked him in the eye. I couldn't tell if he was serious or not. I hadn't talked with Jack Munger since high school, and even then, we were not real close. He liked to get into things that were a lot rougher than cigars and gin behind the church garage.

"Nice to see you too, Jack." I stuck out my hand.

"Isn't that the Davis kid's truck?" He smiled as he

shook my hand. I nodded. "Long time, no see." We walked into the restaurant. Jack was treated like a king. Although others were waiting, we got a seat right away. Jack stopped and talked to almost everyone as we walked to the back booth. As we were sitting down a blond waitress brought over a plate of donuts, a pot of coffee and two cups. I thanked her and she smiled. Jack reached for a donut.

"Jack," I looked him in the eye. "A cop eating donuts?"

"Shut up smart ass." I just smiled and sipped my coffee. "What brings you back to this part of the world?"

"I'm just in town visiting my aunt."

"Goddamn liar. I heard that you got picked clean in Florida and ran out with your tail between your legs." He smiled. "How the mighty have fallen."

I didn't take the bait. "Speaking of which, how is it that the guy who spent his formative years telling the whole world to fuck off, starting with old Hunky McCabe, ended up with this job? I didn't think you could be a cop with a criminal record."

"I don't have a record, you asshole. Yeah, I was picked up a couple of times. They thought that I stole a car over in Ardensburg. I spent the weekend in jail before they found out they were wrong. When I was in the can, I saw the guys that were in there. They were acting like real assholes. Then I saw the cops milling around, and they looked like they were in charge and knew it. That's when I decided that I wanted to be on their side of the bars. So, I got a degree and a job with the force. Five years later Hunky retired and I have been chief ever since. You know it's goddamn funny that you are here right now, I got a paper on you the other day."

"Paper? What kind of paper?"

"Every once in a while, we get requests from other jurisdictions asking if we have seen someone to let them know. Sometimes we do, sometimes we don't."

"Who is it from?" Who the hell could be looking for me? I already gave up everything that I owned. The ex and the bank had it all already.

"Some lawyer down in Florida. I got it on my desk. Came in about a week ago. I didn't pay much attention to it 'cause I didn't figure you were ever coming back here. Lookin' to jack you off for whatever's left, I suspect."

"Trust me, there is nothing left. Are you going to reply to this one?"

"That depends."

"On...?" My mind was working. Was it the bank? Was it the ex? That didn't make sense. Unless they knew about the stash under the front bunk. But who else would be looking for me?

"How about this." Jack picked up a peanut donut and took a bite. "How about we cut the goddamn bullshit and you tell me what we are doing here. You and me ain't exactly long-lost buddies, and you didn't come a thousand miles to bust my chops about these donuts."

I took a sip of coffee and looked him in the eye. "Suppose that I was interested in finding out about someone's past?"

"Criminal?" His eyes narrowed as his cop sense took over.

"Maybe. Let's say he is in a respected profession, say a minister. He appears to be on the up and up but is involved somehow in some things that don't add up."

"What's he into, little boys?" I just stared as Jack chuckled at his own joke. I didn't laugh. His hard cop eyes drilled into mine. "Who we talkin' about here."

"T. Whitman Earle. Over at the Presbyterian Church."

I shocked him.

"Jesus H. Christ, Maxwell, that guy is a pillar of the goddamn community for Christ sake. What in God's name do you think he has done?" He was silent for a moment. He sat straight up in his seat and leaned forward. Sweat beaded up on his meaty face. "I think that you better tell me what's goin' on here old buddy. You suddenly show up at my station, after being gone forever, and accuse a local good guy of some criminal activity, and I have to ask myself some questions. First off is how do you know Reverend Earle? What is your interest in this? In case you don't get it, this is when I shut my big yap, and you are going to talk now." I did. I laid out for him what I knew. I told him about the school. I told him about Aunt Liz and the others. I told him about my conversation with Johnny. I told him about what I knew about Earle. Jack didn't move a muscle.

I ended with my observations. "So, what we got here is guy that blows into town, talks up this fake school, takes local church goers for all that he can and leaves. He got Aunt Liz, and four or five others. If he got the others for as much as he did Aunt Liz, then he has got to be sitting on about a half a mil."

"Jesus, Maxwell. Let me get this straight. You are accusing a minister of raising money? That's what these guys do, bone head. My wife has even given to help that school. I think all that fun in the goddamn sun has fried your brain. Get out of here. You are wasting my time." I started to speak. "Go Maxwell, go now before I find that there is some serious defect in that pile of shit that you are driving." Our reunion was over. If it was possible, being chief had made Jack Munger more of an asshole then he already was.

I stood up and threw a couple of bucks on the table. "Look Jack, something is not right here. It stinks. Maybe the whole thing is legit. If it is, this guy is at least guilty of taking a widow's last dollar. If you think he is such an upstanding citizen, prove me wrong. Why don't you be a goddamn cop and goddamn find out goddamn why I am asking these questions?" Jack Munger was biting into the last donut as I left the Towner. He didn't look up. I climbed into the old Dodge and decided that I had done all that I could in town. I headed the old truck back towards the lake, and the Bella Cosa. I thought that it would be a good afternoon to take Aunt Liz out. I popped a Garcia out of its tube as I eased the truck into the light morning traffic. I struck the kitchen match on the dash and lit the cigar as I waited for the light to change. Driving towards Saunders Point, the pungent smoke filled the cab, and I let my mind wander. Jack was right. I was reading too much into this. This guy, Earle, was just a small-town minister doing his job. This was no more than a case of a bunch of old people putting way too much faith in an outdated institution, and foolishly giving away all of their money. What I should do is drive Liz to the bank, set up a mortgage that would allow her to keep her house, and give her enough money to live on. Then I could spend the next couple of weeks sailing around Lake Ontario and helping her fix up the house. After that, get back to Florida, my writing, and my own life. Problem solved. Self-satisfied, I puffed on the cigar, and watched the rural scenery pass. It really was a beautiful day.

EIGHT

"It is very good to see you again, Mr. Maxwell. To what do I owe this pleasure?" I stood in the cramped church office of Reverend Doctor T. Whitman Earle. He was smiling. I shook his extended hand. Books sat neatly organized on the shelves. I sat across the desk in the chair that he offered as he walked to the door.

"Wendy, I am going to be tied up for a while." He didn't wait for response as he closed the door and returned to his seat. Once again, I noticed that he was the picture of a man of the cloth in a tailored black Brooks Brothers with a yellow silk tie sitting on his monogrammed white shirt. I had seen many pastors in this office throughout my youth; I could not remember any that were as well dressed as this guy. 'You're never going to get rich,' Johnny B. used to say. I should have known then that he was going to be a minister...at least that he was thinking about it.

"Reverend Earle, I would like to talk about my Aunt. She looks like she has been through a rough patch, and as

I have been away for a while, I am a little curious."

"Please, call me Tom. Elizabeth is a special lady." He sat back very comfortable in his surroundings. "She was heartbroken when Bradley died. We spent a lot of time together, talking. She talked a lot about you, Mr. Maxwell. She was proud of you, but it was obvious that she missed you." Ouch. That one hit home. I decided not to respond.

"Reverend Earle. Tom." He nodded and smiled." My aunt tells me that you are very active in supporting a private school over in Africa. What was the name of it? Oxbrown? She says that you are always fund-raising for this school and very passionate about its survival." Earle was silent as his dark brown eyes turned as hard as the sandstone that faced the building that we were in. He stared at me for a full minute. I watched as his facial features softened, and he smiled before he spoke.

"Oxbrown is definitely one of my pet projects. A Mission if you will. It has become a very important mission of this church. Your aunt has joined with many others in their support of this mission. They should be commended for their generosity. As Jesus said when he was by the shore and feeding the multitudes with the five loaves and three fishes, 'Rejoice and be glad, because great is your reward in heaven, for in the same way they persecuted the prophets who were before you.'" He stood and walked over to a file cabinet. From the top drawer, he pulled the same brochure that Aunt Liz had shown me yesterday. I looked on the back. Dot com it said.

"Mr. Earle, I tried to look up this website and I couldn't find it."

"DOCTOR Earle if you please." He hesitated, "There must have been a problem with the server."

"Doctor Earle, I have my laptop here, let's take a look at the website. Then you can tell me more about the school. I might be interested in donating." I reached for my bag. Earle stood and walked towards the door. He smiled, but his eyes returned to hard icy stones.

"Mr. Maxwell, Your financial situation is well known around here. I am sure that you have more pressing places for your resources. It is time to end this meeting. I am due at the hospital." He didn't say anything more and walked out of the building, leaving me holding my bag. I walked out to the hallway and was about to leave when I ran in to an old man. I recognized him as Ralph Treats. We used to call him Old Man Treats when I was a young man. We thought he was old then, he had to be ancient now. From the richest family in Newport, He was rumored to have doubled the family fortune.

"Arnie Maxwell, Hold up." Treats grabbed my arm and stopped me from leaving. "I talked to Elizabeth this morning, and she told me that you were looking into this school thing. It's about damn time I say. Earle keeps bugging me to donate. Oh, I've given him a few thousand, just to shut him up, but he wants more. I told him no more until I get more information on the school. One of my grandsons lives in Egypt, and I was going to ask him to find out about it from there. I am not going to give one more cent until he does." His grip tightened. "You find out what's going on, won't you?" I promised that I would do my best, and after shaking loose from his grip, walked out of the church under the vigilant eye of Wendy the watchful secretary. I had the feeling that she would report this conversation to her boss, 'DOCTOR Earle, if you please.'

I walked back up the driveway towards the old truck. I

decided to go over to the library and find out what Kim found. I stopped at the truck and threw my computer bag on the front seat. As I closed the door, I looked into the side view mirror. Suddenly I felt like a schoolboy, nervous to make a good impression. I combed my hair, practiced the snarl-smile five or six times and then, giving up on that, turned to walk to the library across the street. I froze as the phone in my pocket started ringing. I tried to look like the ring didn't scare me, that I meant to jump up and down in the middle of the street and leaned casually against the side of the truck box as I looked to see who was calling. 'JB Good' it read on the screen.

"Johnny B. is that you?" I flipped the phone open and put it to my ear.

"Arnie, buddy." I laughed. Apparently neither one of us was going to give up on the name thing.

"What's up, Reverend?"

"I just got a call from my buddy Pauly over at the Baptist church. He talked to the Baptists out in Ohio. Here's the thing. As far as they are concerned out there, the guy is real scum. He just disappeared. He had been a beloved pastor for about fifteen years, and he left without even saying goodbye. They didn't even know that he was in New York, and totally surprised that he would be involved with a Presbyterian church. According to Pauly, they said that he was the Baptist's Baptist kind of guy. They said that he was a great minister, but he was also what we like to call a denominational snob. They want to get in touch with him. They seem to have some questions for him. I told him we would get back to them." He hesitated, I kept silent. "Arnie. You there? Does any of this help?"

"It is all very interesting stuff Rev, but I am not sure if

it means anything. It might be helpful, and it might not. None of it really makes sense. I don't get that minister's minister kind of vibe from him. I just left his office, and he seems kind of greasy, you know what I mean? He was evasive, and when I tried to pin him down, he left."

"It makes no sense, Arnie. It is almost a criminal act for a minister to just disappear. I am surprised that they haven't asked the cops to find him. Pauly really wants me to nail this down so he can report back to Ohio. Take it from me it really doesn't make sense. Did you find out anything about the school?"

"Not yet, I was just headed to the library to check that out when you called." I ran down my conversation with Kim, leaving out the fact that I was nervous to see her again. I also told him of the conversion with Earle about the website. "It seems like he was dodging me. He left in a real hurry." I stood and started walking towards the library. "But maybe he just had to go." Johnnie and I agreed that we just didn't know enough, and after agreeing to bring Aunt Liz to Lockport to hear him preach on Sunday, followed by 'an old-fashioned Sunday dinner' with the family, I hung up and walked up the library steps. I caught my refection in the window of the door as I opened it. I was snarling.

NINE

"So, as you can see, Mr. Maxwell, I have searched several databases online, and a couple of books in the reference center, including one old moldy one that Evie found somewhere—she is the only one around that knows where everything is. We could not find any Oxbrown school in Africa. A lot of Oxfords, a couple of Oxbows, but no Oxbrown. When Evie heard it was for you, she even called somebody that she knows at the library over at the university. Are you sure that you have the right name?" I showed her the brochure. "You have got to meet her, or she will kill me. Is that ok?"

"Sure," I said without listening. I was thoroughly engrossed in the papers in front of me, and still reeling from the smile that Kim had on her face when she saw me. Was it my imagination, or was she glad to see me also? I took a deep breath as she walked away and inhaled the scent of White Shadow. I did not remember her wearing perfume yesterday.

"Mr. Maxwell?" I was looking at the book on private schools when they returned. "I would like to introduce you to Evie Kerisplay." The expression on my face must have been evident.

"You didn't expect a black woman did you, Mr. Maxwell?" I stared into the defiant eyes.

"I...Uh..." Boy, oh boy, I am so smooth. I could feel the red rising through my collar. "No, Mrs. Kerisplay, I have to admit that I didn't." She laughed. I shook the outstretched hand. Her short thin frame was covered with a gray cashmere sweater, and a tweed skirt that was very similar to Kim's. Her gray hair was twisted into the tightest bun that I had ever seen. As I looked at these two women, so similarly dressed, I couldn't help but think that there must be a dress code for librarians somewhere.

'I get that a lot," she smiled, obviously enjoying my discomfort. "It is a great honor to meet you, Mr. Maxwell. Mr. Kerisplay and I are huge fans. We have all your books and are anxiously awaiting the next. I have a small display of your books, here at the library. It used to be down here in the main room, but last year, the board made me move it." Another shot. Fame, even small-town-boy-makes-good fame is fleeting when the papers are filled with the accounts of the fall. "Would you like to see it?" I looked into her eyes. They had gone from defiance, to admiration, to child-like excitement in the matter of one sentence. I had no desire to see a shrine dedicated to a world that I could not seem to find anymore, but I couldn't say no.

Originally, the library building had been a private residence. The guy that built it was obviously very wealthy, and the house was huge. When he died, he willed the house to the newly created library association, and it had been a library ever since. Some of the nineteenth century residential features were still evident as we entered the large room on the second floor. There was a huge granite fireplace at each end of the room, and over each was a painting of the original owners of the house. On the far wall, between two windows that over-looked Main Street, the Presbyterian Church and the county courthouse complex, was a small table. On the table, were my three books standing in a semi-circle, around a framed auto-graphed picture of me, clean-shaven and smiling by the ocean. I blushed again and scratched at the beard on my face.

"I found the picture on eBay," Evie said. "Personally, I like you better with a beard." I turned to walk away and looked right into Kim's eyes.

"I agree," she said. I blushed but did not turn away.

"So, tell me about Oxbrown," Evie said. I gave her the same rundown about book research that I told Kim the day before.

"Mr. Maxwell, we are not going to get anywhere if you lie to us."

"Evie," Kim looked shocked. "Why on earth would Mr. Maxwell Lie?"

"I don't know honey, why don't you ask?" She looked me in the eye. "Before you answer, Mr. Maxwell, remember that this is a very small town."

"She's right." I looked at Kim. "But I didn't lie, I just adjusted the truth." I looked back at Evie. "You are a sharp cookie." Her expression didn't change. "The truth is that I didn't want to drag my aunt through the local grist mill. I was trying to protect her." I looked around, noticed that no one was near, and told them both the story. Money, minister, possible crime, they both stood in silence, riveted to my tale as I finished. "So anyway, I am sorry that I lied, but you can understand, can't you?" I looked at both women. "By the way, Mrs. Kerisplay, how did you know that I was lying?"

"My husband. He does handyman work for Mr. Treats. Old Man Treats has been complaining about the minister ever since he got there. One day he was mowing the lawn when Reverend Earle came by. He heard them arguing about money for this school. When I heard you were looking for the same school, I got suspicious. I didn't expect the story that you just told me though."

"Is it true?" Kim looked surprised. "I met Reverend Earle a couple of times and he seems so nice."

"I don't know. All I know for sure is that he has managed to get a lot of money from a bunch of people. Jack Munger practically threw me out of the Towner when I mentioned it to him. Maybe I am crazy, but something doesn't feel right. Munger got angry, Earle ran off when I tried to talk to him, and now you tell me that there is no such school listed anywhere in your references."

"I still haven't heard from the college," said Evie. "We don't have a complete collection. Maybe they know something that we don't."

"I hope so," Kim replied. "Anyway, Evie, don't you think that we should invite Mr. Maxwell to have lunch with us?" She looked at me expectantly.

"I think that's a great idea, Kim. I want to talk to him about doing a reading while he is here." Evie Kerisplay looked me in the eye. It was a look that told me that the only right answer was yes.

"I would love to have lunch with you." I ignored the reading part. "Unfortunately, Aunt Liz is expecting me.

Perhaps another time." I promised to keep in contact with them, and Evie promised to call when she heard from the college. Momentarily lost in Kim's disappointed smile, I left.

TEN

Aunt Liz was standing on the porch when I pulled into the driveway. Although still the same frail woman, she was wearing a plain black dress and her hair was combed and pulled into her signature ponytail. She was sweeping the porch steps. Sailing was a waste of time, she concluded as we walked into the kitchen. What a difference. The entranceway had been swept, and the dishes were all washed and put away. Without asking, she pulled cold cuts and cheese from the refrigerator. I grabbed the bread, still kept in the same drawer, by the dishwasher. As she cut up lettuce, onion, and tomato, I brought her up to speed on where I had been, and what I found out, which was nothing. She listened quietly as we carried everything out to the porch table. I asked her about the others in the church, and if it were possible to find out how much money, we were talking about.

"Way ahead of you. I talked to Peggy Rumson this morning. She said that they gave almost twenty, and she thought that the Lardner's gave almost fifty. I was surprised by that. I didn't think that the Lardner's had that much money." I was surprised too. Already we were at one hundred and seventy thousand. I didn't think that there was that much money in Newport. "I also talked to Ralph Treats," she said. "He wouldn't tell me how much he gave, but I got the idea it wasn't as much as the others. He said he was suspicious about the school and wanted to know more."

"He caught up to me at the church and told me the same thing," I said. "He wants me to look into it deeper, but I don't know what I can find out."

"Well, he didn't get that rich by throwing his money away. Peggy said that they were supposed to give another check this week also, but were not going to give anymore either, until we know more, and she was going to spread the word. Let's eat."

Seated on the front porch, we looked out over the lake as we first made, and then ate, thick cold cut sandwiches. Aunt Liz made one as big as mine, and I watched in awe as she worked her way through it. While we were eating, I told her about my encounters with both Reverend Earle and the ladies at the library. She listened as I presented the negative information. With two thirds of her sandwich gone, she stopped eating. She sat silent for a while. I finished my lunch, turned my chair and looked at the lake.

"That Evie Kerisplay is one of the finest women in town. The library is lucky to have her. They say that she knows where every book in the place is, and has read most of them, even yours." I told her about the shrine. "She is proud to have a local author to show off." She looked over the lake. Seagulls were swarming near the beach. We listened to them cry and watched as they swooped down on a dead fish. "This is bad Arn. What if there is no school? That means that we hired a crook. This will wreck the church."

"The church? What about you and the others? This has already wrecked you. If he is a crook, then we need to find out. Maybe we can recover some of the money. At least Earle will go to jail. If this is what it looks like, he deserves to go jail."

"But he has done so much good for all of us, and for the community." She looked like I had killed her best friend.

"Aunt Liz, we have to face facts, the only thing that he did for this community is to rip off some of the wealthier members." I stood up. "I don't think that that's such a good thing for the community." She started to cry. I felt bad.

"We don't know that," she returned in a small but defiant voice. She looked me right in the eye.

"You're right. We don't know that." I relented and sat back down. We sat in silence as I puffed on my cigar.

"What are we going to do, Arn?"

"I don't know, Aunt Liz. It appears as though there is no school. Tomorrow I will go to Munger and tell him what I know."

"In the meantime, how am I going to live? I am almost out of money."

"How bad is it?" I was waiting for this conversation, all the time dreading that it would be worse than I thought. I picked up the dishes and put away the cold cuts as she went into the house to get her records. When I finished and returned to the porch she was there already with a pile of papers, and checkbook on top.

"I am not really sure how bad it is," she started. "I haven't really paid as close attention as I should." We started sifting through her paperwork. Old bank statements, bills, some behind, mortgage records. I was lost.

It took a while, but we got it straightened out. There was enough cash for the next six months, and the house was paid for. There was also an insurance policy with enough cash value to get another year or so if she was careful. That was good news that bought us time. We could now figure out what the deal was with Reverend Earle, and maybe we could get some of Aunt Liz's money back. And the others. I could feel the tension leave the room as I looked out over the lake, and Aunt Liz went to the kitchen. She returned with a tray of lemonade and homemade chocolate chip cookies.

"I can't remember the last time I baked," she said as she placed the tray on the table. "I hope they are ok." I took two. They were. We put the problem behind us as I spent the rest of the afternoon under her watchful eye working on the neglected yard. Aunt Liz soon tired and took to supervising from the chaise I pulled into the sun. When I finished mowing the lawn and weeding the flowerbed by the back porch, I joined her. After declining her dinner invitation, I hopped into Ol' Betsy and headed back to the marina. My head bounced off the roof, and I almost let go of the steering wheel as I pulled into the marina parking lot. I pulled up next to the telephone booth and headed towards the marina store for a paper. There was a young girl that I didn't recognize behind the counter, and she smiled as she gave me my change. I smiled back and walked towards the dock, a long shower, and tall gin and tonic.

"Mr. Maxwell?" I turned and looked into the face of another young girl. I noticed her sitting on the bench where the dock widened but paid no attention. Her long brown hair hung loosely past her shoulders, and it wasn't until she smiled that I recognized her.

"Kim? Is that you?" This definitely wasn't the same young woman with the bun and the gray cardigan tending to the books in the library. I barely recognized her. She looked beautiful in her 'Newport' hoodie, and a pair of faded blue jeans that fit just right in all the right places. I just stared.

"You didn't think I dressed like that all the time, did you?" She read my mind. I blushed. She giggled. "Oh my God, you did." Eyes fixed on the dock, I nodded, and we both laughed. It felt good. I looked up, into those blue eyes. I suddenly missed the Keys.

"So. What brings you down to the marina?"

She looked me in the eye. "You."

"Me?" I smiled.

"Well. You and Oxbrown."

"You found it?" She nodded and held up a large canvas bag. Funny how I hadn't even noticed that she was holding anything. "Hey. How did you find me anyway?"

"Remember, this can be a very small town, Mr. Maxwell. Everybody knows everything. Evie's son Eli goes to school with young Dale Davis. Dale was in the library the other day saying that there was a guy that brought a boat all the way from Florida. Evie and I put two and two together. Dale said that he thought that you were staying on the boat, so I took a chance and waited. I was going to give you about five more minutes." She glanced at Bella. "That your boat?" I snarled my best smile and invited her aboard.

After giving her the fifty-cent tour, I excused myself to rinse off the afternoon's labor. I thought about how surprised I was that Kim was in the galley waiting for me. I washed as fast as I could and when I returned to the galley, hair still wet and big wet spots on my "Anyone but Bush" sweatshirt, I noticed that she had been busy. Two large gin and tonics stood side by side on the counter. Hers was about a third gone. Next to them was a large plate with thick slices of pepperoni and cheese, and the remnants of an old box of Wheat Thins that she found in the upper cupboard. I winced when I saw them because I knew they were probably stale. She must have brought the pepperoni and cheese.

"I hope you don't mind." She smiled. I smiled.

"Mind? I step out of the shower and the pretty girl has set up a party."

"I found these crackers when I was looking for the tonic. They looked pretty old, but I tossed them into the micro, and they came out fine." I took a bite, tried to chew with a big goofy grin on my face, and agreed. I felt like a fool, but I couldn't get the smile off my face. I took a gulp of gin and tonic. It was perfect. I leaned against the sink, perfectly content. "Don't you want to know what I found out?" She pointed to the bag.

"Did you find it? Did you find the school?" I was suddenly standing again. She nodded.

"I found it alright. Actually, what happened was that Evie found it. She got it from an old book in the travel section. There was a school in Ghana called Oxbrown," she said. I immediately let out a sigh of relief, at least there wasn't anything crooked going on. "Hang on," she said as she read my expression. She pulled out an old leather-bound book from her bag; it was an obscure mission travelogue of Africa, of all things, created by a woman's society of a Methodist church. Evie was good. It also listed private Christian mission schools. She opened it to a pre-marked page. "What she had to do was go up into the attic. That's where we keep all the old volumes that nobody ever looks at. Evie just can't force herself to get rid of any of them, so it's quite crowded up there. I hate going up there, so I don't unless I really have to. Besides, Evie is the only one who really knows what's up there. She was gone for almost an hour. I was getting ready to send a rescue team after her. This book was published in 1914, and in 1914 there was an Oxbrown School for Girls in the Gold Coast Crown Colony, Ghana now, in what is now known as the upper east region. This book shows colonial history of the area from that time and lists the school as a small missionary school run by the Anglican Church. It was about twenty years old at that time. The next volume of this book that we have access to makes no mention of this school. That one was printed in 1931. There is no modern listing of a school by that name anywhere in the world, and I googled missionary school - Ghana, the upper east region, then the country, and there are currently several schools listed as missionary schools, some run by Methodists and Lutherans, and some are funded by Catholic Charities. There are a couple in the upper east region, and both are only about twenty to twenty-five years old." She looked up, waiting for my approval. "Oh, and none have names that even sound remotely like Oxbrown. One was Smithfield, or something like that, and I can't remember the others. Evie said we should assume that the school disappeared before 1931."

I sat down. I had to think for a minute. If there was a school, then the best-case scenario was that an overzealous minister was taking money from members of his congregation that were more than willing to help. A couple of quick conversations with him, and members of the congregation would set limitations and life could go on. But there was no school. He had chosen a name that was obscure enough that it wouldn't be confused with a real school. He was either lucky, or very smart.

"Arn?" Kim's voice broke my stare.

"Kim, you know what this means don't you?" I put the cracker I had been holding back on the counter. I started pacing.

"Yes, Mr. Maxwell," she grabbed my arm to stop me. "It means that in 1931 there was no Oxbrown school in Africa, according to this one book." I stared at her. "I don't think we should jump to conclusions."

"Kim, everything points to the fact that there is no Oxbrown. Not in Africa, not anywhere," I was getting more wound up. "Even Evie says there's no Oxbrown. Anywhere after 1914. We can't find it on the internet, the website is bogus, there is nothing. Fake-ola" I was beginning to pace again. She started laughing. It was a good deep laugh that started deep in the pit of her stomach.

"Fake-ola?" She could hardly breathe. I was just getting started.

"I'm no detective, but it sure looks like this guy's a fuckin' crook, and he took a lot of money from a lot of people. Including Aunt Liz. We should go to Munger right now. He should arrest that phony and get him to get all the money back." I was yelling. I was on a roll. "I am going to call him." I grabbed my phone. "Shit."

"What's the matter?" She was still laughing.

"I don't know his fuckin' number." I started stumbling around the boat looking for my laptop. I could get his number off the internet. I couldn't find it. That started her off again, this time I joined her. We laughed until tears ran down our cheeks. It felt good.

"Maybe that's a good thing," she said. "Let's just stop and relax for a moment. We don't really know anything. There might be more." I started to get excited again. "You said it yourself. We're not detectives. You are a writer and I am a librarian. And this is not an emergency. Tomorrow you can talk with Chief Munger and tell him all we know. He can come to the library, and we will show him the book. He is the police around here. If the law is broken, he will take care of Reverend Earle. In the meantime, there are empty glasses that need to be refilled, and we should walk down to the lake and watch the sunset. It has been a long time since I have been down to the lake."

I felt better. Kim was right. That was the right thing to do. I pulled two insulated glasses out of the cupboard, and quickly made two more drinks. After snapping plastic spill-proof lids on them, we set out towards the lake and the end of the pier. I was looking forward to sharing my happy spot with Kim. As we walked under the marina sign, past the old trees and the diner, out onto the stone pier, our drinks forgotten weights in our hands, she told me a little bit about herself. She was born and raised in Newport; her family went back to the Stone Age. Her great-great grandfather was one of the town founders. Her father was Henry McDermott, and he worked for Mr. Treats running his office. When she was 18, she was dating a guy named Trevor Shultz. Everybody called him Sparky.

"Anyway, Sparky and I were going to get married and spend the rest of our lives together. So, when it came time to go to college, I followed him to Ohio where he had a football scholarship. The school didn't really have the programs that I wanted but I figured what the hell, we were going to be married. I would stay home, like my mother, and take care of the kids. It didn't really matter. So, I took Library Science, bid my time, went to all the football games, fraternity parities, etc. and during our senior year, as I was planning our wedding, I discover him, naked in a room full of cheerleaders. He said he had been thinking it over. I threw a chair at them all and walked out. I have not talked to him since. Sounds pretty cliché doesn't it. Anyway, I graduated, and came back to Newport for the summer. The former librarian, Harriet Lazear, retired that summer, and Evie took her place. She hired me, and I have been there ever since. It's been almost three years now." As we got to the flat rock at the end, and turned towards the sunset, she took a big sip of the almost forgotten drink and finished her tale. "I keep saying I am going to leave, but I don't. No place better to go, I guess." She got quiet and turned towards the lake and the setting sun. We stood together sipping the last of our drinks and watching as the sun dipped into the water at the horizon. Its final rays turning the blue sky first orange and then gold before becoming a small sliver that disappeared into the lake, bringing on the dusk.

I got the desire to leave Newport. I had felt that same desire. I also understood how she had been hurt by this Sparky guy. His way of telling her he wanted to leave was a lot harsher than my wife's, but it was the same story.

When Cindy told me, we were in the kitchen. We had just finished another installment of the argument over money. She just quietly said that she couldn't do this anymore. I moved out three days later. I had tried to be angry with her, but I was just hurt.

Kim and I stood in silence listening to the waves splash against the pier. We both had been hurt in former relationships. In what we thought were spectacular ways. As I stood there, I thought that while they were spectacular to us, they were equally cliché. Neither story was unique in any way, and the only insight that could be gained was that there were other things we should be doing, and other places that we both should be. And with other people. I thought that here, and now, and with her was a pretty good start. I turned to tell her all of this and all I got out was, "Um."

"Hey, old man, I'm still hungry. I haven't been to the diner in a long time, but I remember that they have a pretty good cheeseburger. Wanna take a lady to dinner?" She smiled and looked into my eyes. I was lost again.

"Absolutely." It was clear that whatever had captured her thoughts while the sun was setting had passed. She chatted all the way back to the diner. I only heard about half because I was about five steps behind her, but I didn't mind. I liked the sound of her voice.

ELEVEN

We both ordered medium rare cheeseburgers and a plate of fries that we shared; her half smothered in ketchup. In between bites, I told her my story. About becoming successful, marrying Cindy and spending the next three years living the good life. The house, the condo, the parties, the boat. I told her about the inevitable crash, JerryJack's attempt to make me part of the wall, the unsuccessful attempt to write again. My last trip to Key West. She listened, and asked good questions that kept the tale going, and when I got to the day at the lawyers when I officially gave up everything but the boat, she put her hand on mine and smiled gently.

"The rest, as they say, is history," I said. "I decided that I needed a change of scenery, and Newport seemed like the right place to go."

"I think you were right," she smiled. With that the waitress brought the check. We stopped at the register so that I could pay the bill. She noticed the poster behind the counter. She looked at me, and at the poster. She winked but said nothing. The night air had turned cold, as it can on an early spring evening in Western New York. She pulled the hoodie over her head, and we walked quickly to her car in the marina parking lot. We agreed to meet for lunch the next day, with Evie if she was available, and I agreed to get in touch with Chief Munger so that he could see our evidence. After a big hug, she hopped into her car and drove out of the parking lot. Like a kid, I stood there watching her taillights until they disappeared.

I walked over to Ol' Betsy, and discovered that my bag, with my laptop, was still in the front seat. I grabbed the bag, locked the truck, and headed back towards my boat. My mind was racing over the evening. Over the revelation that there was no Oxbrown school, and the implications that surround that fact. Earle was crooked and had duped several people in the community, including Aunt Liz, and the members of her church, and others. Didn't Munger say that his wife gave money to Earle? I stopped at the bottom of the stairs that led to the dock. I think he did. I continued towards the boat. By the time I climbed aboard and settled into the galley, my mind was on Kim. The remnants of our evening were still on the counter, including the book that she forgot. I could still smell her perfume as I mixed one last Gin and Tonic and cleaned up. When I was done, I moved over to the little dining table that folded away when extra sleeping quarters were needed and pulled my laptop out of its bag. While I was waiting for it to boot up, I took a sip of my drink and lit up a Garcia. The pungent smoke filled the boat. Uncle Bud suddenly popped into my head; he was smiling.

I googled the Newport police department and got the

number for Chief Munger. I put the number in my phone along with a reminder to call him the next day. I didn't think I needed the reminder, but I did it anyway. I was getting ready to close the computer when I noticed that there were some unread emails. I opened the inbox. There were five. One wanted to sell me Viagra cheap, and a second proclaimed that I had won the Liberian lottery and promised twenty million British pounds could be mine if I sent all my pertinent information to this email address. I spam-blocked them. The third was from Johnny Good, confirming that we would see them on Sunday and to plan to have dinner after church. The fourth was from my ex-wife. The subject line read: WHERE ARE YOU, YOU BASTARD. I deleted that one unread. The fifth was from my editor. I stared at that one for a few minutes, my finger on the delete button. 'New Novel" it said in the subject box. I stared at the idea, new novel. I opened it. 'I haven't heard from you in while, old buddy. I hope that means you are hard at work on your new best-seller.' I closed it unanswered.

Maybe it was the soft buzz I felt from the gin, or the warm glow that I still had from my evening with Kim, but for the first time since leaving Florida, I didn't totally reject the idea of writing a new book.

TWELVE

Rain bounced off the deck of the Bella Cosa; it woke me up. Weak gray light filtered through the portholes as I rolled over and looked at my alarm clock. 6:37. I rolled over again, pulling the blankets with me, and listened to the rhythm of drops as they beat on the boat. They were accompanied by the sound of a cool morning wind flowing through the trees. Rustling. I found it restful. What I wanted to do was go back to sleep. I had a slight headache from last night's gin. But I was wide awake. Instead, I decided to start my day with a run. I pulled the blanket over my head, and tried to talk myself out of it, using the weather as an excuse, but I got up, and after dressing and stretching below deck, walked out into the wet morning and up to the parking lot. Once again, I struggled to find my rhythm. I took off on the same three-mile loop I ran the other day and was avoiding mud puddles as I finally hit my stride. I let my mind go blank as I ran. I felt the muscles loosen up. I started to warm up and began sweating the past few days out from my pores. I felt each drop of rain as it hit my face and relished the contrast between the humid warmth generated by my working body and cold damp air. This was a sensation that I never felt when I ran in Florida. I liked it. I picked up the pace, trying to expend every bit of anxiety, frustration, and anger that had been hanging on for the last few years. I ran hard. I wiped the rain from my eyes and pushed as fast as I could until about two miles into it when I hit the wall. I started to breathe heavy, and my legs cramped up. I walked the last half mile and was limping by the time I got back to the parking lot. I cursed both my out of shape body and the desire to push it to the limit. It must have been the cool air, and rain that motivated my sprint. I have always been a casual runner, never looking to push myself. My goal has always been to run just enough to be able to say I was a runner. This morning was different: all the wires and joints were connected. All the gears and belts were properly lubricated; I wanted to run. I wanted to burn out every ounce of energy that I had. I wanted to excise Cindy, and Florida. I wanted to sweat out thoughts of Earle and his fake school, and of guilt over my abandonment of Aunt Liz. I wanted to run through my memories of last night's dinner. It had been a while since I had spent any time just enjoying the company of a woman. I wanted to do it again.

I let the rain cool me down as I walked back to my boat. I went below, stripped off my wet clothes, and stood in the hot shower for as long as I could. As the hot water penetrated my skin, the muscles began to loosen up. I felt tired, but good. I finally stepped out of the shower, fearful that I would run out of hot water, and heard my phone ring as I grabbed my towel. It was only 8:00. The screen read, 'Munger,' the number I just put in there last night. I flipped it open.

"Hello?"

"Jesus Christ, Maxwell, where the hell are you?"

"Jack? How did you get this number?"

"I'm a cop. How do you think I got your number?"

"Ok," I moved into the galley and started to make a fresh pot of coffee. "I was going to call you later this morning. I found something out about Reverend Earle."

"Yeah, that's one reason I called. I heard you were still snooping around in that mess. But that's a small pile of shit now. I'm gonna ask you again, where are you?"

"I'm on my boat. Down at Davis' marina. What's the problem?"

"Don't go anywhere. I'll be right there." He hung up. What the hell was that all about? I poured a cup of coffee and finished getting dressed. I decided to meet him up by the store. I filled a go-cup with coffee and headed back out into the rain. This time it just felt cold. I was sitting at a picnic table under the front porch overhang facing the parking lot when the cruiser pulled in. Munger got out, and so did the thin deputy that I met the other day. Dickenson, I think his name was. As I watched them walk across the parking lot, all I could think of was the Laurel and Hardy movies I used to watch with Uncle Bud.

"Maxwell."

"Hey Jack. What happened, did they run out of donuts in Newport?"

"Cut the crap, smartass." He didn't look happy; he looked tired and a little grumpy.

"Dan, how about you go and get us all a cup of coffee." I watched him as he talked to Dickenson. He looked at the deputy as if he were a younger brother following him on a date. He was in the way. Dickenson hung his head and went inside the store. I had the feeling that he wouldn't be back out until Munger had finished telling me whatever it was he came to tell me.

"So, to what do I owe this great honor?"

"Ralph Treats is dead." He stared at me looking for a reaction. Treats was an old man, and I didn't know him very well. I didn't react.

"What?"

"Treats is dead."

"What happened?"

"Still trying to figure that one out. He was found on the floor in his bedroom with a big dent in the side of his head."

"What's that got to do with me?" He looked me in the eye.

"I suspect foul play."

"Holy shit." I stood up and walked to the edge of the porch. "Who would do such a thing to an old man like that?" He didn't answer my question, he just continued to stare. I walked to the other end of the porch and back. His eyes followed every step. It hit me.

"Me?" I yelled. "You think it was me? You came all the way down here because you thought it was me?" I quickly went back to the conversation I had with Treats in the church. That was the first time I encountered him in at least 15 years. I couldn't remember the last time I talked to him. There was nothing about our conversation that was in any way confrontational. In fact, I would categorize it as amicable. I stared back. "You gotta be kidding me."

"Let's just say your name was mentioned and leave it

at that."

"What the hell does that mean? My name was mentioned. My name was mentioned? Who the hell would mention my name? Who even knows that I am here? Why the hell would I kill Old Man Treats?" I was getting angry. No one likes being accused of murder, let alone first thing in the morning.

"For the love of Christ, Maxwell, how in the hell would I know. All I know is—you show up here unexpectedly. You start snooping around, raising questions about a guy that has done a lot of good around here. At the same time, I get a couple of requests to call the authorities in Florida if I see you. Next thing you know, I have the first murder in Newport in anyone's memory on my hands, and near as I can tell, you are one of the last to see him. As a cop, I gotta say, put all that together and it begins to smell. Real bad. Looks like you left Florida in a hurry. You didn't tell anyone you were leaving or where you were going. Maybe there is something going on down there that I should know about. Maybe you were running." He sat down at the table. "Maybe I ought to lock you up and then call them down there."

"Look Jack, I know you are a great cop and all, but people don't go around killing each other around here. Isn't it possible that he just fell, and hit his head?"

He ignored the sarcasm. "Right now, all we got is a dead man on the floor with a lot of blood. We can't find what he might have hit his head on. There are no sharp corners or objects in the house covered with blood. Whatever hit him is no longer there. Whoever did this, took the weapon with him. I asked his daughter to tell us if anything was missing. She lives next door. She couldn't find anything missing. Whoever did this, brought the weapon with him also."

His eyes were hard as nails. All of a sudden, he was looking at a suspect and was searching for a way to gain an advantage. "Where were you last night?"

"You gotta be kiddin' me." My cell phone rang. "I was right here on my boat." It was Aunt Liz. I ignored it. I would call her back later. "How exactly did my name come up?"

"While we were there last night, your buddy, Earle showed up. Apparently, Treats' daughter called him. He told young Danny in there that you and Treats were talking at the church yesterday. He insinuated that it was not a friendly conversation. He said you argued." He pulled out a small notebook. "So, you say you were on the boat last night? Anybody with you?"

"Munger, I shouldn't have to tell you anything, but I will. First of all, I did talk with Treats yesterday. Aunt Liz told him that I was checking into the school. He shook my hand, told me that he wasn't going to give Earle any more money, and encouraged me to keep looking. As for last night, I was here last night, on my boat with Kim McDermott. We had a couple of drinks and went to watch the sunset. We stopped at the Baited Hook for dinner, and she went home. She got here about six and left about ten." He flipped open the notebook. I got the idea that he already knew the answer to that question. I wondered how.

"That sounds right. So how is it that an ugly old cuss like you got a pretty little thing like that McDermott girl on your boat?"

"I was at the library, asking about Earle's school. She found some information and thought I would like to know. She showed up unexpectedly. Something stinks here, Jack.

But it's not me." He looked like he wanted to blast me into next week. I guessed that it had been a long night for him. "There is no school in Africa. No Oxbrown."

He put his head in his hands. "What the hell are you talking about? I told you the other day to stay away from that shit. My wife gave to that school." He looked up again, and the hard cop eyes bored a hole into mine. "I ain't got time for this shit, Maxwell. That was the other thing I came to tell you." He put his hat on and stood up. "Let it go. I don't need some smart-ass writer wanna-be coming into town and shakin' things up." He walked over to the door. "Dickenson. You dumbass. Are you grinding that coffee in there?" He looked back down at me. "You know who else has a thing for that librarian?" He tilted his head toward the door where Dickenson was paying for two cups of coffee. "Got it bad. Thing is he's got a big fat bitch of a wife, and a whole pile of kids. Works mostly nights to get away from them. He stops by the library all the time. That librarian is pretty smart. She won't have anything to do with him. It's kind of a sore subject. The guys at the police station give him shit about it all the time."

Dickenson walked out with the coffee. Munger took the cup from his deputy. They exchanged a look I didn't understand. I noticed that he only brought two. "What you should do, old pal, is be a good little boy and leave the police work to us. Just sail that nice little boat around the lake, visit your aunt and do whatever it is you do, and when you have had enough New York, just point it south again and go home. Otherwise I might just remember that I saw you around here when I am near those phone numbers in the office."

"Numbers. There's more than one?"

"Yeah, I got a second one from a detective in Fort Lauderdale. I don't give a shit if your wife's divorce lawyer is looking for you, but now the cops down there are interested. I don't feel right not calling them. You better fix that, and quick, or I'm gonna."

"Why so sour, Jack, did you miss breakfast?"

"Don't crack wise, boy-o. Take this as one old friend giving advice to another old friend." He hopped into the car and Dickenson spun the tires in the gravel as the cruiser pulled out of the parking lot. I sat at the picnic table and looked out over the morning as the sun started to peek out through the clouds.

What was that really all about? Why would Munger travel all the way out here to see me, and tell me in person that Treats was dead? He knew where I was last night and knew who I was with. It didn't make sense that he would come all this way to confirm what he already knew. As I figured, Earle's secretary must have reported the conversation with Treats. I didn't think she was in ear shot, but maybe she was. I wondered who came up with the idea that we had argued: her, or him. Whoever it was, why would they think we had argued? The only reason I could come to was that someone was trying to pass suspicion for Treats' death onto me. Perhaps away from himself? I wondered if Earle just offered the info, or only after Munger asked. I should have asked. I wondered what hit the poor old guy. I wondered if there was any connection between Treats' death and our conversation. As I stood up to walk back home, the sun disappeared.

It hit me just as I entered the galley. Something wasn't right. Everything was in the right place except for one cupboard door. I walked over and looked at the slightly opened door. I know that it was closed before because every cabinet door on the boat had a safety latch installed so that the doors would not swing open when the boat was in heavy seas. They were like the childproof latches that would allow the door only to open enough to get a finger in and press the spring-loaded clip that held the door from opening. They were made of plastic, and this one was broken. Someone had been here. I started to look around. Whoever it was had done a good job of covering their tracks, but it was clear that someone had done a thorough search. I got mad again. I opened my phone. I was going to call Munger. It had to be his deputy. Maybe that was why he came down. Was he looking for the murder weapon? He said it was missing. But why would he do an illegal search? Why didn't he just ask? I snapped the phone shut. Something wasn't right here. I ran back to the bedroom. I pulled my little steel box out from under my bed. All my cash was still there. It didn't make sense. If Munger thought I was a suspect, he would have gotten warrants, and kept any search that he did on the up and up. I decided not to call him. I wasn't sure why, but all of a sudden, I didn't trust my old buddy anymore. Satisfied that nothing was taken, and solid in the belief that Dickenson had been the one that did the search, I put my money back under the bed, and went to take a shower.

By the time I sat down at my little table, it was raining again. As I opened my cell phone to call Aunt Liz, I was stopped with one more thought. I couldn't get the thought out of my head that there was more going on here. Munger was right about one thing. It all smelled real bad.

THIRTEEN

Aunt Liz's voice mail said that she wanted me to come over right way. She sounded stressed, and I was immediately sorry that I didn't take her call. I grabbed the keys to Ol' Betsy and for the third time this morning set out into the rain. I felt kind of funny doing it, but I wanted to know if anybody else had any interest in my old boat. I took a small hair from my beard and stuck it on the outside of the galley door. It seemed a bit over dramatic, but it was all I could think of. I remembered as a kid seeing James Bond use this trick in the one where he went to Jamaica. I had a couple of hours before I had to meet Kim for lunch, and I wondered if that would happen. A guy as prominent as Treats dying upsets the whole community, and rumors that he was murdered amps up the buzz. I bounced in the seat as the old truck splashed out of the parking lot. The windshield wipers only smeared the water onto the windshield. I could hardly see. Aunt Liz's house was quiet as I pulled into the driveway. The early morning wind had died off, and the rain hit a flat lake.

I wiped my feet as I walked in the door. The house was spotless, like I remembered as a child, and I automatically removed my shoes. Aunt Liz yelled that she was in the kitchen, and that I should go out to the front porch. When I got there, the table was set with coffee cups and homemade blueberry muffins. I didn't realize until that moment that I was hungry. Aunt Liz walked in with a coffee pot; she was already dressed and made up. After a hug and kiss, she poured two cups without speaking. We sat down.

"Ralph Treats is dead." That was the second time this morning that I had heard that.

"I know. Jack Munger came to the marina this morning."

"Now why would he come all the way down there just to tell you that?" I took a bite of muffin. It was still warm. I told her about our conversation. I left out the fact that Dickenson had gone through my stuff.

"He thinks Ralph was murdered?" She looked skeptical. She stood up and looked out over the lake. "Why does he think that? Who would do such a thing? What does he think you had to do with it?"

"Reverend Earle told him that Mr. Treats and I argued yesterday at the church."

"What were you arguing about?"

"We didn't argue. Mr. Treats said you told him I was looking into Oxbrown and encouraged me not to stop until I found out the truth. I promised him I would. Besides," I cut a second muffin in half and covered both halves in butter. "Earle wasn't even there. He left, and the only other person around was his secretary."

"Wendy Pearson. I never trusted her. She was hired right after he started. She seems...shifty. I am not sure that's the word I want, but I just don't trust her." She sat down again and picked a muffin. "Sure, I talked to Ralph. He called to ask about a new member. What made Tom think you two had argued?"

"I've been wondering that myself. Either she told him that we argued for some reason, or he came up with that one on his own."

"It doesn't make any sense. You wouldn't kill anyone, let alone Ralph Treats," she said. She started to pick up the table. "Anyway, we gotta go." All of a sudden, she was all business. "I want you to take me to town so that I can visit Emma Treats. See if there is anything I can do. I don't like driving in the rain. Then I gotta meet the ladies at the church. I am sure that the funeral will be there. We have a lot to do." She put her coat on. I got out my keys. "We're not going in that thing. Get my car out of the garage."

FOURTEEN

Emma and Ralph Treats lived in an old brick Victorian on the north side of town. They had lived there forever it seemed. The story on the house was that a local judge once owned it. He was good friends with Franklin Roosevelt, and when Franklin was governor, he and Eleanor used to visit. It was set off the road by a large front yard. A cast-iron fence, covered with ivy vines, hid it from the bowling alley across the road. We pulled in and had a hard time finding a place to park the car. Three other cars and a police cruiser were in the driveway. As we parked by the old garage, a deputy that I didn't recognize came down the back porch and headed towards the cruiser. We locked eyes as he pulled the car out of its spot. I helped Aunt Liz across the driveway, through a small garden, and up the stairs to the back door. She knocked but didn't wait for an answer.

As we walked into the living room, I noticed a big old photograph framed and hanging over the fireplace. It was a picture of the porch we had just walked in on. I didn't recognize most of the people, but there was a young FDR and Eleanor standing with the others. After expressing our condolences to Mrs. Treats, and a bunch of people that I didn't know, Aunt Liz told me to get lost. I was a little disappointed; I wanted to look around. I wanted to see the bedroom. Try to figure out what hit him. She said that Mrs. Lardner was there, and she would give her a ride to the church. She would call me, she informed me, when she was ready to go home. I walked out and stood on the top step. This was the step where Franklin and Eleanor Roosevelt once stood. As I thought about that, I looked out over the small garden between the house and the back yard. It was mostly covered with dry leaves and dead vegetation left through the winter from last spring. In one corner was an old cast iron birdbath that had been painted white at one time and needed to be repainted. On the left side of the birdbath moving away from the back corner were four posts buried in the ground. These posts were black and looked like tall, thin Academy Award statues. They were buried at different heights with the closest one being the same height as the birdbath, and, on the last, only Oscar's head and shoulders were visible. On the right, there were five. The last on that side only showed Oscar's head. I thought that was strange, but maybe with plants growing around it made sense. I pulled the Olds out of the driveway and headed into Newport.

After leaving Aunt Liz, I drove over to Wal-Mart. I had some time before I had to meet Kim and wanted to get a new pair of wipers for Ol' Betsy. As I headed toward the automotive section, I was rewinding parts of the day. It was not even noon, and it was already packed with more activity than the last couple of weeks combined. I was by the photo section when I remembered something that Munger had said. The Fort Lauderdale police were looking for me. What would they want with me? When I left, everything was signed, sealed, and delivered. Cindy had the house and most of the earnings from my writing, both past and future. The lawyer had the rest. All I had was the boat and the money stashed under the bed. All mine, mostly legally, but not worth any undue attention. I didn't think anybody even knew I had it. I decided that when I got home, I would call my friend Sarah Murphy, a detective on the Lauderdale force, and see what was going on. She would tell me and keep it on the QT.

When I was at the height of my success and words were flowing out of me like water, people were throwing money at me. I lived the good life. I used to stop at the Wal-Mart that was on the way to Key West and laugh at the guys that were standing in the parking lot with their old trucks, their hoods open, working to keep their old wrecks running for another week. As I walked back to Aunt Liz's car in the rain, I recalled one guy that had crawled right inside of the engine compartment of an old Chevy pickup with no windshield. Only his feet hung out, barely touching the ground. I don't know what was wrong with the truck, but he must have fixed it, because the truck started with his head still under the hood and rolled, over one of his feet, across the parking lot into a brand-new Cadillac. I watched with shock, as the guy just left the truck still crunched into the caddy, still running, and walked away, limping.

How the mighty have fallen. I was one of those guys now. Home was a 38 foot sailboat. Everything I owned was onboard. The wife had taken everything. When I got home, I would be standing in the parking lot of the marina fixing an old truck I didn't even own. The Volvo was gone. I was sure that if Cindy saw me now, she would laugh and say something about getting what I deserve. I don't know, maybe she was right. Back then, I had it all. Nice house. Pretty wife. Fame. Fortune. I blew it. I let it all go. I quit working, my misguided ego believing that at any time, I could just open a laptop and whip off another best seller. I lived the good life. When it came time to go back to work, the best seller wasn't there. I had nothing. I couldn't even come up with a bad idea. Nothing. I don't know if I deserved it or not, but I surely brought it upon myself.

With that idea, I got into the car. I had only myself to blame. Through the years, I tried blaming Cindy. I blamed my parents, I blamed Uncle Bud and Aunt Liz. I blamed editors, and agents, but it wasn't up to any of them to keep writing. It wasn't their job to do the work. It wasn't them who got lazy. It was all on me. Now I was standing in the rain in a Wal-Mart parking lot in Newport, buying wipers for a truck I didn't even own, and it was all because of me. I threw the wiper blades into the backseat and climbed in. I drove towards the library. At least I had that to look forward to. The thought of Kim's smile made me smile. I wiped the rain from my face and looked at my watch. I had ten minutes to get to the library. I was morose and soaked. This was not going to go well.

I sat in Aunt Liz's car outside the library. It was parked across the street, in front of the Presbyterian Church, and I could see the front door from where I was. I wanted to dry off a little before going in. I also wanted to get over the sour mood. As I sat there in the car, on Main Street in

Newport, feeling sorry for myself, I remembered something that Aunt Liz said to me when I was ten, and we had just buried my parents. Sometimes, she said, things don't go the way we want them to, but they always go the way they are supposed to. I didn't believe her then, and I wasn't sure I believed her now, but as I got out of the car and headed towards the library, I hoped that she was right.

I ran up the sandstone steps and pulled open the thick oak door. I walked into a silence that is only found in libraries and empty churches. It blended perfectly with the smell of freshly cleaned antique wood and books. No one was there to greet me as I walked into the main lobby and up to the reservation desk. I looked around. Evie had moved the display of my books back down to the main room. I looked at my shaven face staring back at me. It seemed to look right through me. I shivered.

"There you are." I heard Evie before I saw them.

"You're late." Kim walked around the corner into the fiction room with Evie close behind. She sounded stern, but she was smiling. "We have lunch prepared upstairs." We walked up the stairs and into the big front room. They pulled a table into the middle of the room and set it with a tablecloth, paper plates and plastic cups. There was a tray of submarine sandwiches and a two-liter bottle of Pepsi.

"I hope this is ok," Evie said. "I don't like to leave the library in the middle of the day. Debbie, the children's librarian downstairs, will watch the front desk while we eat. This is your seat." I sat in the chair that faced the window. Outside was a breathtaking spring view of the Newport courthouse square. The rain was letting up again, and the sun sent individual rays peeking through the clouds. The copper dome top of the courthouse glowed as a single ray seemed drawn like a spotlight. It seemed like the perfect spot to eat lunch.

We made small talk, mostly about Ralph Treats' death, as we ate. We all knew pretty much the same stuff. The murder rumor was flying around town. I didn't tell them about my visit from Munger. The subs were delicious. I was shocked to hear that Kim had made them herself. "Much better than any shop around here," she boasted. It wasn't until we were finished with the meal and Evie returned from taking care of a couple of phone calls in her office, that the conversation changed.

"I talked to my friend over at the university this morning," Evie started. Kim and I both turned and looked at her. "He confirmed that there was no school specifically named Oxbrown anywhere in Ghana. Not even in Africa. Although there is one in New Zealand. Are you sure that the school we are looking for is in Africa?" I nodded. Kim pulled out the brochure that I gave her the other day. There was no street address, but it was clear that this school was in Africa. Kim and I both got excited at that statement. Evie had just confirmed what we already knew. We started talking loudly and at the same time. Neither was listening to the other, and Evie had to yell to get us to shut up. When she finally succeeded, she asked one simple question. "Why?" We both stopped and stared at Evie like she had a third eye. "Why would Earle do this?"

"It's obvious, don't you think?" I spoke first. Kim looked at me and nodded. "He is a con man. He thought he found a small town full of ignorant rubes and he is trying to fleece them." Kim nodded.

"No," she said. "That part is obvious. Even to a po' ol'

black woman like me." Evie liked to slip into an old-fashioned black stereotype whenever she talked about herself. I wondered why and decided that it didn't fit. "Arn, when you two were caterwaulin' here a minute ago, I thought I heard you say that he was a respectable minister out in Ohio. What I am wondering, is how does a respectable minister move from one job in one state to another and all of a sudden become a crook?" That one stopped us in our tracks. We debated this question back and forth. Maybe he got into alcohol or drugs, or worse, and needed money. Maybe he snapped under the pressure. Kim assured us that this was possible as she saw the disbelief in both Evie, and me. She told us of a minister in the next town who told his wife he was taking the computer to be repaired and was found three days later in Ohio, at a strip joint. He claimed that he didn't know how he got there which was possible as they found two one-liter bottles of gin in the trunk, empty.

I started telling them about Johnny B's conversation with his friend, Reverend Pauly. I decided not to tell them about Munger's warning. Although Johnny didn't tell me much, the fact that Earle split in a hurry from Ohio seemed to fit into our conversation. Evie brought up a good point. Why, was the question that I hadn't asked yet. The whys were piling up. Why was this guy doing this? Why did he change from an upstanding man of the cloth to con man? Why did he leave Ohio so suddenly? Why did he come to Newport? Where was the money?

"Why don't I ask him? I'll just stop by the church and ask him." I picked up my cell phone. "Let me see if he is there." I dialed the church office.

"First Presbyterian church, this is Wendy speaking."

"Wendy, this is Arn Maxwell. Is Reverend Earle in? I would like to stop by and talk to him."

"Doctor Earle is not here today, Mr. Maxwell." I wondered if she was covering for him. I decided to just go over there when I hung up. "In fact, I haven't heard from him at all today." Her voice trailed off. She sounded wistful, like an unsure lover. She quickly recovered. "Is it important? I can give you his cell phone number?" I wrote the number down, and after thanking her, hung up and dialed the number she gave me. I got his voicemail. It said he was unavailable and gave the church number for emergencies. I hung up without leaving a message.

As I was looking at the silent phone, Evie spoke up. "Mr. Maxwell, as nice as it is to have you here with us, we do have to get back to work." I looked at her, and at Kim, with some disappointment. My phone rang. It was Aunt Liz. She was ready to go home, and I had to come and get her at the church right away. I hugged both of them, and at the last minute, asked Kim if she would like to go sailing the next day. She smiled that great smile and immediately said yes. For the first time that day, I smiled too, my snarl noted by Evie, who was nodding her approval. I walked out onto the sandstone steps of the library and stood for a moment. I felt good. I fished in my suit coat pocket and pulled out a Garcia. I lit it up and pulled the first drag deep. I looked to see if the sun was still making the courthouse dome glow, but the sun was behind the clouds. It seemed very bright anyways. I decided to leave Aunt Liz's car where it was and walk around the church and down the driveway to the office. Picking up Aunt Liz at the church was good. I could kill several stones. I could talk face to face with Wendy, and if Earle was there, I could confront him too. Puffing in the cigar, I waited at the intersection for the light to change. Slowly I crossed Main Street, and walked up the sidewalk, past the car and the church. I could smell spring. I walked down the driveway, and before entering the back door, I carefully put the cigar out and saved it for later.

FIFTEEN

I walked into the little vestibule outside the church office and could see through the window that Aunt Liz was sitting in the office talking with Wendy. I could not hear what they were saying, but the conversation seemed serious. When I approached the door, Aunt Liz stood up, gathered her purse, and waited for me to enter. I looked at her and at Wendy. Wendy was sitting behind her desk.

"You remember my nephew, Arn?" she looked at Wendy.

"We met the other day," she said, not looking up from her task. "And he called earlier today. Before you ask, Mr. Maxwell," I was looking down the hall toward the pastor's office. "The answer is still no. He has not been here today."

"She doesn't know where he is; do you dear?" On the surface, Aunt Liz sounded like she was concerned. I remembered that tone from when I was a teen, however, and realized that she didn't believe Wendy, and Aunt Liz was still pumping her for the answer she expected.

"It's not like him not to tell me when he is not going to be here. I had to cancel his whole morning." I was about to make a snide comment about how hard that would be, when she looked up. She looked distraught. Aunt Liz shook her head to stop me.

"I'm sure he is ok, dear. He was up late last night, and probably is just home sleeping." Wendy didn't look convinced and picked up the phone as we walked out of the church.

"Why don't you have him call me when he gets in touch?" I said and held the door for Aunt Liz.

On the way home, we talked about Ralph Treats. Calling hours were Monday. The funeral would be Tuesday. Aunt Liz was coordinating the reception after-wards. She sounded awed when she said there was a chance that the governor might come. We talked about his death. They still hadn't figured out what hit him. Nothing seemed to be missing, and there was no forced entry, but they couldn't find any place in the house that looked like he hit his head. Munger was confused. They apparently spent most of the morning searching the grounds but didn't come up with anything. The sun was trying to take command of the sky when we pulled into the driveway. I offered to help her with some yard work, but she begged off. She was tired and wanted to rest. I parked the car in the garage and headed in Ol' Betsy back to the marina. The sun had gained control, and as I walked across the parking lot, I relit the Garcia in my pocket. I quickly replaced the wiper blades and grunted with satisfaction as they flopped back and forth across the glass. I operated the washer, and they cleaned every bit of the blue liquid off the glass. Feeling good about that, I headed down the path toward the lake, not really thinking about anything. I was just enjoying the spring warmth of the sun and watching as the wintered world surrounding the Oak River began to come to life. Geese were flying overhead. Northbound: headed in the right direction, as Uncle Bud used to say.

I walked out onto the end of the pier. The wind had shifted and was blowing warm air from the South West. Clouds floated by. There was rain out on the lake, but the offshore breeze kept it out there. I watched as it slowly moved past me. I tried not to think. I just wanted to be in the moment. The lake was smooth, and geese were landing about a hundred yards away. Their honking blended with the soft rustling of leafless trees on the bank. Spring blended with the smoke from my cigar, and I decided that there was not a more perfect time, or place, in the world. I sat down. My mind wouldn't stop.

I guess I didn't know what I expected when I decided to make this trip. Maybe I retained a romantic view of the area through the years, everything perfect and orderly, but the truth is that all the time I lived in South Florida, I never even came close to any criminal activity. I come home and here I am in the middle of two possible crimes, with the cops warning me to stay away from one and suspecting me in the other. I thought that everything would be the same as when I left. This idea sounded naïve, even to me. I realized that all my adult life, I had been driven by naïve ideas. Maybe it was time to grow up. Maybe it was time to get my act together. Be a man; quoting Uncle Bud again. This place was in turmoil, and I had stumbled into it. I decided that I didn't want to be a part of it all. I would let Munger sort out the whole mess. I decided I would follow his advice. I would just work on getting to know Kim better and helping Aunt Liz get her house in shape. She was going to have to sell it at some point. I would then sail around the lake a couple of times, and then back to Florida. Maybe I could get some writing done when I got back there, or find a job doing something.

With that decision made, I felt better. I headed back to Bella. It was Friday night. I wanted a big drink, and steak. I decided to have a drink at home and then go over to the Old North for dinner. I poured a large gin and tonic. I tossed the empty gin bottle into the trash and made a mental note to get more on my next trip to Newport. I felt good. With nothing to worry about, I could concentrate on my sailing excursion tomorrow. It was one of those April evenings where the air was almost warm enough to sit outside, so I pulled a sweatshirt on and moved all my stuff out to the picnic table that was on the dock. I took a big sip and opened my laptop. It was still early in the Lake Ontario boating season, so Bella was one of the only boats in the marina. It was quiet and with my hood up, I was very comfortable.

There was only one email this time, from Cindy, my ex-wife. Again, I deleted it, but it reminded me that I was going to call Sarah Murphy. I walked back to the boat and got my phone. Sarah was a detective on the Fort Lauderdale police force, and many years back, before I forgot how to write, I asked her to help me with some research about drug lords in South Florida. We spent an evening drinking Heineken and eating raw clams in a bar by the river, and she advised me to stay away from them. I followed her advice and we have been friends ever since, spending many evenings in that bar drinking Heineken and eating raw clams. I dialed her personal phone.

"Maxwell, is that you? Hang on I'm having dinner with some friends." I heard rustling, and muted apologies as she moved to a quieter location. "Where the hell are you?"

"Maybe I shouldn't tell you until I know why you are looking for me."

"How did you know I was looking for you?"

"Maybe I shouldn't tell you that either."

"It's not me looking for you, it's Cindy. Something about your boat, and some money. JerryJack has her all wound up." JerryJack was Cindy's brother. Last time I saw him he tried to force me through the living room wall headfirst. Cindy sent him home before he could do any real damage. I didn't care if I ever saw him again. "Look Arn, I'm not getting in the middle of this. This is something that you have to work out with her, and I know you will. But you need to talk to her. She is driving me crazy looking for you. I finally put up a request, just to shut her up." She was silent for a moment. "That's how you knew, isn't it? You're in New York."

"Yeah. I am sitting on a dock on the Oak River, looking at the Bella Cosa, about a half a mile away from where I grew up. I had to get away. One of the guys I went to school with is the local chief. And he told me that you were looking for me."

"Look, Arn, I gotta get back to dinner. I'm not going to say anything to Cindy about this call as long as you get things straightened out."

"I'll talk to her," I said. "I'll call her on Monday. I got some things going on this weekend." She accepted that and hung up. So, Cindy was looking for me. But why didn't she just call? I decided that I really didn't care. I looked out over the water. A pair of ducks was swimming up the other side of the river. The sun was setting. It was peaceful. I opened the Word program. An electronic blank sheet of paper stared back at me. Daring me to type. I did. Everything that had happened in the last few days spilled out onto the empty page. I wrote for an hour. After correcting my spelling errors, I re-read it. It read like a cheap murder mystery: small town minister bilks old ladies out of their life savings and murders to cover it up. It had to be the truth, it sounded too cliché to be a decent piece of fiction. I saved it and closed the laptop. It was dark and chilly, and I was hungry. I decided to go get something to eat.

SIXTEEN

The drone of a small outboard engine woke me up. The sun was already up. I looked at the clock, 8:45 am. Just opening my eyes made my head hurt, and waves from the fishing boat rocked Bella just enough as it passed. I barely made it to the bathroom and vomited in the toilet. As I lay on my bathroom floor with my head resting on the sink, I tried to get my brain started. Last thing I remembered was the waitress taking my dinner plate and telling me that the people at the other end of the bar wanted to buy me a drink. I was clearly hung-over but couldn't remember any of the rest of the evening, or how I got home. With one arm wrapped around the toilet seat, I fell asleep.

SEVENTEEN

I awoke on the bathroom floor. My whole body hurt. I wasn't sure how long I had been there. I felt like I was ninety as I walked into the galley. 10:00 am. I could think a little. I made a pot of coffee and tried to remember last night. I left here and drove over to the Old North Inn. There was a wait for tables, so I ate my dinner at the bar. The steak was perfectly done and accompanied by a baked potato and a large green salad. I drank Labatt's and felt like I had the world by the balls. There was even a hockey game on the television. All I needed was a cigar, and the night would have been perfect. I decided to go back to Bella, grab a cigar and another beer, and walk down to the end of the pier to watch the sunset. The plan was to make it an early night. I wanted to try some more writing in the morning, and Kim was coming in the afternoon.

What was that old saying about best laid plans? Mine changed just as I paid my bill and was finishing my last beer, when a group of bikers walked in. With their long hair and leather, I immediately tensed. I had never known anybody that was a part of that culture, but I had seen many biker movies and was looking at the stereotype. Like all stereotypes, this one was busted as I eavesdropped on their conversations when they moved into the empty spot at the bar next to me. Instead of being the ignorant thugs I expected, this group defied everything I believed about bikers. Educated and intelligent, they figured out who I was very quickly. Apparently, the news that Arn Maxwell, bestselling author, was in town had spread, and one biker chick was especially excited to actually meet me. She wanted to go back and get her copy of *Outside the Dreams* until she was reminded that her book was thirty miles away at home. I tried to leave but they insisted that I stay and have a drink with them. At this one chick's insistence, she said her name was Betty, I agreed. Biker Betty, I tagged her. One more beer wouldn't hurt. I could still make the cigar, sunset, and early night plan. One drink turned into many, and I had fuzzy memories of shots of Jack Daniels, some dancing, and a late night, high-speed ride on the back of the biggest, shiniest, Harley I had ever seen. Biker Betty was driving. Seems she wanted to show me to her friends. I don't remember any friends. As I took my first sip of coffee, I tried to remember more. How did I get home? Where was Ol' Betsy? What happened after the bike ride? It was all a blur. I walked out and sat in the cockpit. The morning sun was hazy, and clouds were rolling in, but it was just warm enough to sit there and vegetate. The fresh spring air smelled clean. I slowly sipped my coffee. I felt terrible. I had to do something. Kim was coming in a little while. It looked like another rainy day, and all I wanted to do was go back to bed. I went below and poured another cup of coffee. I grabbed my cell phone and decided to cancel my afternoon date with Kim. I called the number she gave me and left a message saying that I wasn't feeling well, and that we should go sailing another time. As I put the phone down, I figured it was probably better that way. If the plan was to go back to Florida, it seemed fruitless to get involved with Kim. Besides, this morning it seemed like way too much effort. I closed up Bella and walked up to the store. I needed aspirin, and I wanted to see if the truck was there. I walked around the front of the store so I could see the parking lot. The truck was parked neatly in the corner by the dumpster. I grabbed the keys out of the ignition. I went into the store, bought a bottle of Advil, and a pack of Alka-Seltzer. I went back to the boat and after drowning the aspirin in a half-gallon of orange juice and a large fizzing glass, crawled back into bed and for the second time that morning went to sleep.

"Hey Maxwell, you in there?" Someone was thumping on the side of the boat. "Let me in." I tried to open my eyes. A girl's voice. More thumping. "You gonna let a girl stand out in the rain?" I opened my eyes. My head didn't hurt so bad. My stomach felt ok. I looked at the clock. 4:38. The thumping got louder. "Hey! I know you're in there." The voice sounded familiar. I rolled over, deciding that whoever it was could go away, when it hit me: It was Kim. "Come on, Arn. It's getting cold out here." I jumped up and pulled on a pair of sweatpants and a t-shirt. "It's about time." She was soaked, but she was smiling. She was wearing an oversized yellow rain slicker, and her hair, darkened by the rain, was stuck to her face. She looked beautiful. I wondered how long she was out in the rain before I heard her. She placed two large plastic bags on the counter, another on the floor. "Not feeling so well?"

"Yeah, I must be coming down with something." I didn't want to tell her that I was hung-over.

"Could it be the Jack Daniels flu?" she looked at me. There was a smile in her eyes.

"Now, how in the hell could you know about that?"

"You don't remember?"

"No, there is a lot about last night I don't remember." I blushed. I looked her in the eye. She laughed. "Oh God. What did I do?"

"You called me." Oh man, this can't be good. There should be an automatic drunk button on cell phones, maybe a breathalyzer tube. If you blow in the tube, and your alcohol content is too high, the phone won't work. It would save a lot of embarrassment. "You told me that you couldn't find your keys. You wanted me to come help you find them. It was two-thirty in the morning." Oh, shit. "My cousin Jimmy owns the Old North, so after I got off with you, I called him. He said you were wandering around the parking lot yelling for your keys. One of the bikers took them away from you before you went on your bike ride. Jimmy and one of his dishwashers brought you and your truck home. He then called me and told me that you were going to be a hurtin' puppy in the morning, but that you were home safe."

"Kim, I am sorry..." She held up her hand. She was laughing.

"After you called this morning, I decided I wasn't going to let you off the hook that easy. You gonna play, you gotta pay right? But now it's raining so we can't go sailing anyway. They say it's a big storm coming across the Midwest. Should be here for a few days."

"We could go out on the lake if you like." I didn't sound excited. I looked at the counter. "What's in the bags?"

"I thought that since you were treating me to a ride on this wonderful little boat, I would treat you to an amazing dinner." She opened the first bag. She pulled out two thick strip steaks, a bag of potatoes and baby spinach. From the bottom of the bag, she pulled out tomatoes, onions, garlic, a couple of plastic bottled spices, and herbs. She smiled sheepishly." I didn't know if you would have everything I needed." I didn't. From the other bags came a bottle of Plymouth gin, a two-liter bottle of Schweppes tonic, two limes, a loaf of bread, and mozzarella cheese. "We will have all summer to cruise in this old tub. There's no sense in going out on the lake if all we are going to do is sit in this cabin." I looked out the porthole by the kitchen sink. It was still raining. It almost looked like night. She was right. "What you should do, you old drunk, is to go and get presentable. You cannot entertain a lady properly in sweatpants and a smelly old t-shirt." She was laughing as she shooed me off to the shower. I liked it.

I stood in the shower and washed off the final remnants of last night. I was feeling a lot better, and even though it was raining, I still couldn't remember every-thing, including the phone call, and my head still hurt, but Kim was aboard. I could hear the clanking of pots and pans in the galley. I wrapped a towel around my waist, and quickly trimmed up the beard, and brushed my teeth. I combed my still wet hair back off my face, parting it on the left side. I ignored the growing hairless spot on the top of my head. I peeked out the bathroom door. Kim's back was to me, so I made a beeline for the bedroom. I put on my cleanest pair of LL Bean khaki pants and a brown polo shirt. I slipped on my most comfortable Old Navy flip-flops. Unsure, I looked down at my feet. "She's just going to have to deal with it," I muttered aloud. I walked out into the galley.

Kim was cutting up slices of tomato. She looked up from her chore. "Now that's what I'm talkin' about." She smiled. I melted. She walked around the counter with two gin and tonics. She handed me one. We clinked glasses and both took a sip. Perfect. She had been busy. On the end of the counter, the two steaks sat seasoned and resting on a platter. The whole counter was covered, as she was creating. Spinach, bread, cheese, tomatoes, onions, mushrooms; all were set out in various forms of preparation. I was impressed. I opened my laptop and opened up Pandora. I chose Van Morrison and plugged in the Bose speakers that I had mounted on the bulkhead. I put speakers throughout the boat, including a couple of waterproof speakers on the deck by the door to the galley. I flipped the switch to inside, and "Brown-eyed Girl" filled the air, adding to the general party mood.

"All right mister. No time to dawdle. I assume you have a grill. These steaks deserve real charcoal." She looked me in the eye. She was having fun. "You are in charge of that. Hop to it." I laughed as she shook the knife in my direction.

I got to work. I dug the grill out of storage. It was a small black steel pot that fit onto a bracket that was attached to the railing in the cockpit, right next to the wheel. I put my slicker on and went out to screw the grill into the bracket. I didn't have any charcoal. I ran up to the marina store and bought a small bag of Kingsford Match Light. I also bought a lighter. I walked back to Bella, placed the bag of charcoal in the grill, and lit it. The air was damp, and the bag was a little wet, so I had a hard time getting the fire started. Persistence finally won over the rain, and I got the heavy paper lit. I watched as it burned and ignited the charcoal. I closed the lid and went back inside.

I shivered as I went below. It was warm inside. Once again, this was a feeling that I had forgotten. Living in Florida it was always cooler coming into any building. I walked into the boat from the cool damp outside air. It was warm, and the smell of food cooking pervaded every inch. It all felt very domestic with the little woman hard at work. I hated myself for being a little old fashioned, but I liked that part. Kim was pulling a tray out of the oven filled with small slices of toasted bread covered with melted mozzarella cheese and tomatoes. I could smell the basil that covered them. She set them on the counter, searching my face for approval. She got surprise.

"Well?" She said. I took one. It was still hot. It was delicious. Surprise turned to approval.

"That is good." I took the paper towel that she handed me and wiped the small string of cheese out of my beard. I ate another. Kim chuckled and clucked like a mother hen, happily returned to her project of creating our feast. She made small talk as she worked. I sat at the table and tried to keep up. She was talking about people and places that I didn't know, but I was interested anyway. I think that she could have read the dictionary, and I would be enamored. I made us both another drink, and we finished the appetizers as I told her about my trip up from Florida. Using my writer's skill for detail and embellishment, I kept her laughing as I recounted different characters and events that I encountered over the month-long trip.

"It's time," she said. She picked up the empty appetizer

tray and put it in the sink. "Let's see if you are any good with that grill." She handed me the plate with the steaks on it. I put my slicker back on and, after grabbing a cigar, headed outside, steaks in one hand, gin and tonic in the other. The charcoal fire was perfect, and the strips sizzled as I put them on the grill. Two minutes each side to sear, then five minutes more each side should do it. I looked out over the trees and saw a break in the clouds. If that kept up, it would be a nice sunset. I sipped my drink, sat in the cockpit, and bundled up against the weather.

EIGHTEEN

One of the skills that I was especially proud of was cooking. Especially on the grill. Taught by Uncle Bud from an early age, he used to let me light the grill, and when I was a teenager, he let me do the cooking. That lifetime of experience was completely expended on those two strips, and they were perfectly done. Kim broiled sliced potatoes with olive oil and rosemary. She also tossed the spinach with tomatoes and the remaining mozzarella cheese. She blended her own vinaigrette. It all meshed into the best meal I had eaten since I left Florida. I dug out a bottle of Yellow Tail Shiraz, and we toasted good fortune. It was as if the rest of the world didn't exist. Only Kim, and me, this boat, and this moment. I was happy. As we emptied the small bottle of wine, I told her about my decision to let Munger handle the whole Earle mess. He could do with it whatever he wanted. I would hang around for the summer, sailing around the lake, and help Aunt Liz get on her feet. Then probably go back to Florida and try to jumpstart my career. I told her about writing yesterday, and how good it felt. She was silent for a moment. Then smiled. I looked into her eyes. They were blue. No, not just blue, but the only time I had ever seen that color blue was when I was in Key West looking out over the ocean. Our eyes locked for a few seconds. It felt to me like a lifetime. She blushed and turned away.

"Mr. Maxwell, You certainly showed your prowess cooking these steaks." She held up a glass of wine in a mock toast. Plates once filled with rosemary potatoes, and spinach salad lay empty on the table. She made just enough. The only thing left untouched from her bags, was a bottle of Leonard Oakes Fuji Apple wine. It made the perfect desert. We sat in a comfortable silence, each sipping our wine for a few minutes. Kim was the first to speak.

"Evie called while you were out cooking the steaks. She said that Chief Munger came by the library today." She picked at a crumb of potato that was left on her plate. "He wants Evie and me to bring him everything we have about that school. I don't know what we can tell him. We didn't find anything."

"Maybe he is wising up."

"He also told her that no one has seen Reverend Earle since he was at Treats' house the other night."

"Well, he will be around tomorrow. Munger should be able to catch up to him at church." I had to admit that I wasn't really interested in talking about Earle. Having decided to let Munger handle it, I turned my thoughts to helping Aunt Liz. "I'll come with you on Monday, and we will tell Jack everything we know." Surrounded by the remains of the evening and filled with a couple of glasses of good wine, I was feeling just right. I changed the subject slightly and told Kim about what I wrote yesterday. "Nobody would believe it as fiction," I ended my tale. "It sounds like something John MacDonald would have thrown away." Kim looked at me. It didn't register that she might not know who John MacDonald was. She finished the wine in her glass.

"All right mister let's get this mess cleaned up." She took a handful of dishes over to the sink. I followed with more, and as I approached the sink, she turned around. In the small boat, we were face to face. I looked into her blue eyes. For what seem to be a lifetime, we stared into each other's eyes. I set the dishes on the counter, and I kissed her. She jumped. Oh, Shit. I stepped back.

"Kim..." I was going to apologize; try to save the evening. She put her finger on my lips.

"You startled me..." She put her arms around my neck and kissed me. Amazing. Soon we were arms around arms. Lips on lips. Our tongues attempting to share every bit of passion that two people can create. I kissed her neck and ears. She moaned. She held me tighter. This went on for several minutes until I took her hand and headed towards my stateroom. We stood at the end of my bed; I looked into that beautiful smile as slowly I peeled her hoodie over her head. As her face re-emerged, she wasn't smiling anymore. The expression on her face was pure passion. She might have quit smiling, but I was snarling ear to ear.

Throughout my life, I could count the number of lovers on my hands. I was good with that. I always believed that the quality of the experience far outweighs the score-keeping pleasure of quantity. Living with that philosophy, anticipation has always been one of the most exciting parts. Seeing, exploring for the first time, reveling in the newness. Standing here with Kim, as layers of clothes and layers of inhibition were peeled away, anticipation built to the level of Christmas morning. As we stumbled through abandoned clothes and fell on the bed, our eagerness grew, and we explored each other completely with our mouths and hands. Searching for that spot, seeking the next one, moving together, moving apart, searching to find each other. Giving, taking pleasure, once, spending, being spent, only to be fueled again; using knowledge gained, and seeking new knowledge until we lay spent and sweat-covered on top of the covers. Silent, in our own thoughts, nestled as close as two could be, sleep overtook us.

It was pitch black when I opened my eyes. It took a few minutes for them to adjust to the frail moonlight streaming through the portholes. By that time, the warm wet pleasure that I felt on my stomach had moved lower. Fully aroused, I watched as Kim's mouth slowly and softly took me in, it felt great. Just as I was ready to explode, she stopped, her eyes closed, and moved on top of me. I closed my eyes and took pleasure in this girl, who was seeking, and clearly finding pleasure. We moved together, in perfect rhythm, building, closer, deeper, and faster, until in the quiet of the Oak River night, at the same time, with the same cries, released. I grabbed her hips and pulled her as close as I could get her. I wanted to be a single being, totally connected, feeling, thinking, knowing, as one. I never wanted that moment to end. Purring with satisfaction, she rolled over, snuggled into my shoulder and with a light peck on the cheek, went back to sleep. I soon followed.

When I woke up again, the morning light was just

beginning to loosen the night's hold on the world. I rolled over; the bed was empty. I lay still listening for the sounds of movement but got none. Still naked I walked into the galley. It was cleaned up, and the bags were gone. Was I dreaming last night? I looked around. After the laughter and pleasantness of Kim's visit last night, after the smells of girl, and good food, after the awkward moment that preceded our lovemaking, after the late-night round two, and the most pleasant way ever devised to wake a man up, Bella was empty. She looked sullen and forlorn. I felt the same way. There was a single sheet of paper on the counter; I picked it up.

Arn,

First of all, let me say that although last night was wonderful, I did not come with the intention of staying the night. As the evening wore on, I happily and willingly succumbed to your charms, and I hope you know that I am not the kind of girl that jumps into bed with every good-looking, boat-owning author she sees. I hope you don't mind that I woke you in the middle of the night. I just needed... well you get the picture. You got the picture. You got everything else too...lol. Having said that...this is a very small town, and it would not do to be seen leaving the marina, crawling home on a Sunday morning. Call me when you get a moment this afternoon. This morning I will be in church. Hopefully staying awake... and thinking of you.

K.

It was signed with a big scrawling K that took up the rest of the page. Well, it wasn't a dream. I re-read the note several times and decided that I would in fact call her when I got back from Lockport. I grabbed a cup of coffee and went out to watch the sunrise. It was early yet, and I didn't have to pick Aunt Liz up for a couple of hours. We were going to go over to John Good's church in Lockport, and then have lunch with his family, on their farm. I decided to go for a run before picking her up. I looked around and saw a small boat coming down the river. I decided I better go inside and put some clothes on. I pulled on the sweatpants and dirty t-shirt that I had on when Kim arrived yesterday. Using Ol' Betsy's tailgate as a leg bar, I stretched out in the parking lot, and started out down the road. I ran past an old couple walking their dog, and then tuned everything out. Concentrating on the feeling of running, the cool wet air, the heat generated by my action, I wasn't tired. I did not sleep much last night, but I felt invigorated. Kim's soft naked body popped into my head, and I decided I couldn't wait to get back from Lockport. I would invite her back tonight. That was all I thought about while I ran.

NINETEEN

I was still going strong when I rounded the curve heading towards the marina parking lot. Once again, I passed the old couple, their dog deep in the weeds. They were headed the other way. I decided not to expend energy running around the big puddle at the entrance of the parking lot and ran right through it. The cool water felt good. I slowed to a walk and started walking in circles around the parking lot. I was breathing hard, my shoes were wet, and my legs were covered with mud, but I felt good. As I cooled down, I walked past the marine store, toward the dock, and a hot shower. I had to hurry a little, we had about an hour's drive to Lockport, and Aunt Liz didn't like to be late for church.

"May I have a word with you, Mr. Maxwell?" The words stopped me in my tracks. Reverend Earle was sitting at the picnic table where I had talked with Jack Munger. He was seated with his back against the building and, lost in my own thoughts, he went unnoticed. "That is, if you have a moment." He was dressed as he was the other day. Once again, the suit looked impeccable. The little white dove standing out against the black of his lapel. I must have been staring at him. "It's Reverend Earle, we met the other day?"

"Of course. I guess I'm just a little surprised to see you. Aren't you going to be late for church?" I wondered why he was here.

"I have plenty of time, Mr. Maxwell. They aren't going to start without me." He chuckled at his own joke. "I thought that we should have a talk, face to face. Kind of, clear the air, as it were."

"What's on your mind?" I sat on the bench opposite him. I stayed towards the other end in case I had to get out real quick. I couldn't quite pin the feeling down, but something was telling me not to get too close to this guy. "You caught me by surprise. I don't have a lot of time, as I too, have to get ready for church."

"You, Mr. Maxwell? Going to church? What a pleasant surprise." I noted the sarcasm and waited for him to speak again. "Well, it will be nice to see that Liz won't have to sit alone this morning. It will be good to look out and see you both among the congregation."

"Actually, we will be going to another church this morning. And as it is a little bit of a drive, and Aunt Liz doesn't like to be late, I need to keep moving. What was it you said you wanted?"

"Another church? Lockport perhaps? Isn't the minister over there from Newport? Good, I think his name is." He looked at me knowing he was right. "Yeah that's it. Wasn't he a friend of yours?"

"Not that it concerns..."

"Concern? Mr. Maxwell, I always like to keep an eye on

my flock."

"Reverend Good is a friend of the family and invited us to spend the day." I looked at my watch. "Now, I am sure that you didn't come all the way down here to discuss my Sunday plans."

"Quite right, Mr. Maxwell." His smile never left his face, but his eyes hardened. "You have been stirring up the pot, Mr. Maxwell. Causing me some trouble."

"Is that what you call it? I am just asking a few questions. Trying to find the truth."

"Seems to me, more than that. All of a sudden, people are not so responsive to my requests to help that poor and deserving school. And now poor Ralph Treats is dead."

"You think I had something to do with all of that?"

"Jack Munger seemed to think so. Especially after I told him that you had argued with him." Earle confirmed what I already suspected. I decided that I didn't need to tell him that I had talked with Munger. That he had cleared me with some simple investigation. I caught him looking at me searching for a reaction. I was ready. I kept a poker face. We were headed towards something, and I was waiting until he played his cards. I decided to up the ante just a little.

"Maybe he found out what everybody is learning. That the school doesn't exist." I looked at him for reaction. He didn't move either.

"I assure you, Mr. Maxwell, of two things. First is that the school is very real, and in need."

"Prove it." I interrupted. I couldn't believe that the guy was holding onto this story. In the wake of all the evidence that was building, he was still trying to work the con. I struggled not to react. I wanted him to think that I believed him, at least a little. "A website, an address, alumni, anything."

"The second thing is that I don't for a minute think I have to prove anything to you. My business is with the members of my congregation, and my community, of which you are neither. Now, as you say it is getting late, and I need to say what I came to say." His whole face changed. Hardened. This was not the face of a benevolent man of the cloth. This was a face that would be at home in a prison. At that moment I believed that he was capable of anything. Even the death of an old man. "Mr. Maxwell. It is usually not wise for people to get involved in things when they don't know all the facts. Very often in that situation someone gets hurt."

"Is that a threat, Reverend?"

"Of course not, Mr. Maxwell. I am merely offering an observation. Here is my suggestion. Enjoy your vacation. Spend time with your aunt. Sail that dinghy around the lake a couple of times, and then head back to where you came from. Leave the rest to me. Let me decide what's best for my church. It is for the best. Really." That was the second time in the past couple of days that someone had said that to me. "Anyway, I must not be late. Have a good week. Pay attention to my advice." He walked over to his car. I hadn't noticed it parked between the dumpster and Ol' Betsy when I ran into the parking lot. Without speed or haste, he pulled onto the road and headed towards Newport. I turned towards the store and looked at the clock on the wall outside the screen door. I was going to have to hurry.

TWENTY

I was in fact late picking Aunt Liz up. It was only ten minutes, but she had the car out of the garage and running when I pulled into the driveway. She was sitting on the porch, upright, purse on her lap. Her face said it all. She wore another black dress, this one fit her perfectly, and her hair, makeup and posture had changed. Unlike the woman who sat on her front porch my first day back, she looked completely alive. I sipped my coffee and only half-listened as she lectured me about the responsibility of being on time. Nodding as she spoke, I went back over Earle's visit in my head. It seemed unreal. As I drove west on Route 18 farther from Bella and the marina, I couldn't decide whether he had threatened me or not. I decided not to tell Aunt Liz. She had ended her lecture and sat silent as she looked out the window.

As we cruised down route 104 and crossed the county line, she started telling me about a conversation she had yesterday with Libby Paine. Apparently, while going through her sister's stuff, she found out that Cathy was also contributing to Oxbrown. Quite a bit. Libby was unaware. So, she was calling everyone to find out what she could. Libby always was the practical one. "As she was calling around, the general consensus was that there was something fishy going on. She talked to Jim Lardner and Betty Clinton, and they both said that they were not going to give anymore until they knew what was happening. They made it sound like no one was. Betty wants to convene the session, without Earle to take action. I told her you were looking into it, but she already knew."

"Did any of them tell Earle about their decision?"

"Libby said that she called Tom and demanded to know more about the school. She apparently threatened some kind of action, maybe legal, if he didn't either produce info about the school, or give the money back. He told her to check with him next week and hung up." The more into this conversation she got, the more animated she became. "Maybe we can get my money back."

"Let's not get too excited just yet." We weren't going to see any of that money. I didn't think that he would just roll over and give the money back. To admit that he even had any money was to admit that he had committed a crime. But the well was drying up. He had to be getting nervous. That might explain the visit this morning. If the con was going sour, he was either going to do something stupid, or he was going to run. I didn't see him as being stupid. My money was on running. As we pulled into the Lockport church parking lot, I wondered why he hadn't run yet. I also wondered how much of this Munger knew.

The April sun was shining on the sidewalk in front of the Lockport church. It was almost noon, and the day had turned into one of those spring days in Western New York that punctuates the end of winter and promises that summer is on its way. Not quite 70 degrees, the sun felt hot on my shoulders and after the last dong of the church bell subsided, I could almost hear new leaves bursting from their buds. I swear I could see the grass turning green. Standing with Aunt Liz and Lynda Good, we waited as Johnny greeted everyone as they left the church. I was proud of my friend; he looked in every way the part of a minister. Right down to the robe that showed wear and the stole that was signed by every member of the con-gregation. It was a gift, he said, from the congregation when he was installed. Aunt Liz held the youngest Good as Lynda tried to corral the others, trying to herd them all towards the car.

I surprised myself. It had been years since I was in a church on Sunday morning. I enjoyed the service. Enjoyed watching Johnny work. The sermon was about redemp-tion. But they are all about redemption. The good ones make it work by making you feel good about your whole life. With the good ones, the line is- man is not perfect, but if he tries to live in a good and honest way, if he believes in God, then he is on the right path. A good minister knows his job is to guide mankind. To teach. The good ones try to make the Sunday morning experience a positive spiritual one. Uplifting is a well-worn word in this setting, but it fits. When I leave a service, I want to feel uplifted. The bad ones, and there are more bad ones than good, especially the bible belt crowd that believes that everything is wrong and spare no expense of pulpit time telling folks how bad they are. The bad ones are interested in tag lines. Verses of the bible taken out of context. Give your life to Christ. Be reborn. I am not a big believer in organized religion because too many good, hard-working people believe these preachers. This leads to people that call themselves Christians yet have the belief that in the name of God, they can kill doctors, or Muslims, or Gays, or anyone that doesn't fit into the Sunday morning mold. The problem is the media, or the other political party. Find the right verse and from the pulpit, justify racism, or homophobia. The bad ones seem to forget about the turn the other cheek, help your fellow man thing. They amend the 'love your neighbor' part to 'love your neighbor as long as he or she acts, looks and believes just like you.' As I listened to the thought, compassion, and creativity that went into Johnny's service, I realized that he was one of the good ones. I like the good ones.

Aunt Liz had gone on ahead with Lynda and the kids. I hung out with Johnny until his work was done and he was certain that the church was going to be locked up. He said there was a Buildings and Grounds meeting going on, but that Old Ben would lock up. Whoever Old Ben was. The women had gone in Johnny's car and left us Aunt Liz's Olds. The conversation was mostly directions as it took several turns and forks to finally get onto the Lockport-Olcott road. We turned left onto Jacques Road and into the first driveway. The old farmhouse faced the main highway. Johnny told me that this part of the road was known as Corwin Corners after two brothers that had originally settled here. They were both buried up the road, in a cemetery that also bore their name.

The kids came running from the back yard, and as we walked around the house, we saw Lynda and Aunt Liz sitting on the back porch in two old wicker rockers.

Although they had just met, they were talking as if they had known each other for years. They looked out over a large backyard, where the kids were chasing a large golden retriever, who was chasing them right back. Under a clump of large Elm trees was a round picnic table set for lunch. It was just warm enough to eat outside. We solved world problems, caught up, and got to know each other over pulled pork sandwiches, homemade macaroni and cheese, and a fresh green salad. The kids ate most of the mac and cheese, and then were herded into the house by Lynda and Johnny for some quiet time. When Johnny returned, he brought two Labatt's, declaring a beginning to his weekend. Aunt Liz excused herself to see if Lynda needed any help in the kitchen. Again, I noted how old-fashioned it felt to have the women in the house taking care of the domestic things. Again, I felt slightly embarrassed by the fact that I liked it. I handed Johnny a Garcia, and we both lit up. As the dog chased some unseen creature out of the back yard, we looked out over the back yard and talked about old times.

TWENTY-ONE

It was good to talk with Johnny again. With everyone else in the house, it was as if we had never been apart. We laughed about some of the crazy things we did as kids. We both agreed that we were lucky that nothing bad ever happened. He told me about how he decided to become a minster, and how he came to be in Lockport. I told him of the writing career, which he followed closely. I also told him about the end, losing everything, not being able to write anymore, and the decision to sail back to Newport. I told him how good it felt standing on the pier. "I'm still not sure why I came back here. I will probably go back in a couple of weeks."

"Of course, you came back home," he said. "Where else would you turn in times of such turmoil?" Same thing Aunt Liz said. I walked around the tree a couple of times, silent. I sat and took a sip. Johnny's eyes never left me. "You should find a nice girl and settle down." I gave him the edited version of my new relationship with Kim.

"There you go." I didn't say anything. Johnny's life was so perfect. Good job, house, family. I was envious. After watching me for what seemed like a lifetime, Johnny finally spoke.

"I talked to Reverend Pauly yesterday." I looked him in the eye. I knew we would turn to this eventually. I was enjoying the afternoon too much, and Johnny was just waiting for the right time. "We met for coffee. He wanted to come over this afternoon and talk to you personally, but he was leaving right after church to go on vacation. He had a lot to tell me." I sat up. "He got a call yesterday from Ohio. A guy named Reid. This Reid is a member of Earle's church out there. Apparently, Reid was talking with the new minster who mentioned Earle, and the fact that he was in New York. The minister had Pauly's number, so Reid called him. It seems that Earle was there for about fifteen years. He had a reputation of being fair, and spiritual. The congregation was growing. There were a lot of upset people when he left without saying goodbye." He took a sip of beer and continued. "It looks like he left after church on Sunday, and Monday was his day off. He was very strict about not being bothered on his day off, so people got in the habit of leaving him alone. He had meetings on Tuesday so was out of the office most of the day; by the time they got around to looking for him, it was Wednesday morning. Reid said he had no family, lived alone, so when it got to Thursday afternoon, and he hadn't been seen, Reid called the local cops. They all assumed that he was the victim of foul play, but the police couldn't find a body, or evidence of violence. That's where the investigation stalled. It was inconceivable to any of them that that he would run, but that was the conclusion that police came to. With no record, or idea that he might be guilty of impropriety, they closed the case, it's not illegal for a grown man to leave town." He paused. "He was very interested in the idea that Earle might be in New York."

"I hope they are talking to the police now. Did he say whether there was a school scam out there?"

"Pauly asked him that. He said that Earle was trying to get something going. He was trying to get contributions to start a school, and a few had contributed, but Reid himself hadn't. There was a couple out there that wondered, but didn't pursue it after Earle left, because the members of the congregation believed he was probably dead. Apparently, they had a memorial service and everything out there."

"Did Earle get much money out there?"

"Pauly didn't say. I can ask him. He was looking more into Earle than the school thing. Before you ask, he didn't get the name of the school that Earle was working with out there."

"How about a picture, did we get a picture?"

"Reid said he had to get one from the church. He was going to send it to Pauly, this afternoon, or tomorrow. Pauly said even though he was going to be on vacation, he was taking his laptop. He would watch his email and send it as soon as he got it. As soon as I get it, I will forward it to you." He stood up. "I'll be right back. I just want to make sure everything is ok." He left me sitting alone in his back yard. Good minister, good husband and father. Good man. I looked out over the large yard, and the farm fields that extended as far as I could see. My mind wandered to those two brothers, Corwin, I think he said. I could see them seated in a similar spot looking out over the same land, their land. Perhaps with a cigar, worried about the weather, the cost of seed. I turned back to Earle, just as Johnny returned with two more beers.

"Maybe it should be gin," I said as I took the cold bottle.

"Yeah," He laughed. "And maybe we should be sitting behind the church garage?" We both laughed. "Those days are gone, my friend. I have a couple of beers now and then, usually on Sunday afternoon. The start of my weekend, right? I don't think I have had any gin since those days. I never did like it much." I laughed. I like it just fine.

"So, where were we," Johnny said as he sat back down. He picked up his cigar, and soon we sat in a cloud of pungent smoke. "I don't smoke these too much anymore either. Lynda is going to complain for a week that everything smells like smoke. It doesn't of course, and she will get over it." He was smiling. I got the sense that it wasn't really a problem. "So, what do we know?"

"Let me try to sum it up." I stood up and took a deep drink of my beer. I walked to the end of the porch. "For fifteen years, Earle worked at a church out in Ohio. He was by all accounts a Baptist minister's Baptist minister. Respected by his congregation and community. His first church? Maybe, maybe not, but judging by age, I put him in his forties, if he had another before that it would have been a short stay." I started pacing, small trail of cigar smoke following. "Respected man of the cloth leading his congregation, he stumbles upon this school in Africa, or a school somewhere, we don't yet know whether it was the same school, or not. Without that information, we cannot tell whether the first school is real, and the mission legitimate."

"It makes a difference whether it was legitimate, or

not, don't you think? It speaks to the character of the man. It sounds like Reid was saying that he was trying to start a new school."

"I think you're right. Was he working on a legitimate project? Did it start that way? The pivotal point in the whole story is the moment that he left Ohio. No explanation, no goodbyes. No forwarding address. Just gone. How does that play into the school thing? If it is the same school, then someone found out and he skipped. If it is real, then why did he skip?"

"It doesn't add up. Why would a guy with such a solid reputation, and standing in the community all of a sudden create a fake school, start bilking his congregation, then skip town?"

"Drugs?"

"You've seen the guy up close, Arn. Does he look or act like a guy that is on something?"

"I'm no expert, but no. I didn't see any erratic behavior when I talked with him. He was quiet, evasive, got angry when I started asking questions. He walked out the first time we talked. Otherwise, he appears to be completely in control. So, say the Ohio school was legit. Say, at that time he was still doing good. Why did he leave?"

"That is the million-dollar question. In many ways, being a minister is just another job. You go to work each day, and you have someone, or most of the time, a board of members that you need to satisfy in order to keep your job. The ideal goal is the same as any job: you search for the right mix of compatibility and challenge, and board satisfaction. But the difference is that a minister's inter-action tends to have a profound effect on the members of their congregation. We come to be seen as members of the family. Hell, we preach that we are all members of the same family. Under the best conditions, the departure of a long-term minster can be troublesome. One who slinks away in the middle of the night can destroy a church. Pauly said that the new minister out there is still working day and night to rebuild. Even if the guy is legit, leaving like that is irresponsible." Johnny had jumped up and was pounding the picnic table as he spoke. "Maybe more so. If he's a crook, it makes sense."

"Alright, Reverend." I laughed as he settled back down in his seat. Johnny was still shaking his head. "Where was I? So, he leaves Ohio, and winds up in Newport. The Presbyterians just happened to be looking for a minister and he applied. He gets the job, even though he is a Baptist, based on above average sermon skills and promises to do great things. In Newport, he resurrects the school idea, this time with a fake school in Africa. A couple of things bother me here, first of all, these people are not stupid, why didn't they look into it?"

"I think I know, Arn. From everything that you've told me, Earle sounds like a very charismatic guy. There are a lot of charismatic people in the ministry. I am always wary. But I also know that the church in Newport had been looking for a long time. Put those things together and you have a guy that everyone wants to believe."

"So, they bought his story, hook line and sinker. Isn't that a condemnation of the whole system?"

"It is definitely the kind of occupational landmine that a good minster will work to avoid, and the rest exploit. The thing that bothers me is, how was it that the Newport church didn't know about the Ohio thing. The process, if you follow it, is pretty intense."

"Aunt Liz said that he was from Ohio, she got that from Jim Lardner. They must not have talked to anyone out there. Let's ask Aunt Liz..." As I was getting ready to suggest that we ask Aunt Liz, she came running out of the house. She had her cell phone in her hand.

TWENTY-TWO

"Aunt Liz?" It was clear that something was wrong.

"Arn, it's Betty Clinton." The pain in her face was growing. Tears were forming. "They found her dead in her living room." Betty and Aunt Liz had been friends for as long as I could remember. When I was a kid, she and Uncle Bud, would always be doing things with Betty and her husband Don. She started to sway, I moved to grab her before she fell, and made her sit on the picnic bench.

"What happened?"

"I don't know. I just got a call from Amy Lardner. When the Clinton's weren't in church this morning, Amy called to see if they were ok. When they didn't answer several tries, she sent Jim to check on them. George was just sitting there. He found her. The police are there now." Aunt Liz started to cry. "We have to go."

We said our goodbyes and after a quick prayer from Johnny, we left. Aunt Liz sat slumped against the passenger side door, crying and mumbling to herself as I drove down Route 104 towards Newport. My mind was filled with questions, but I let her have her moment, choosing to keep my thoughts to myself as she absorbed the idea that her friend was dead. The big question in my mind was whether Betty died of natural causes.

The trip back to Newport was uneventful. I called Kim. Yes, she heard about Betty. She wasn't real close to the Clintons, but was sorry. Evie used to play cards with Betty. Kim was going to go over to Evie's and make sure she was ok. She invited me to her house for dinner, but I said that I thought that I should stay with Aunt Liz. Aunt Liz said I should go, that she wanted to stay with Betty's family for a while, so Kim agreed to pick me up at the Clinton's house in the Clover Heights section of Newport. Aunt Liz could go home when she wanted, and I would get home by myself. That settled, we were all satisfied. I felt sorry for Aunt Liz. Sadness was not just evident on her face; it permeated her whole being. Once again, she looked like the old lady standing on the porch my first day back. I realized at that moment why she looked that way. Sadness had created this frail old woman. That same sadness was evident on the back porch, and I was at least in part, responsible. I decided right then and there never to leave her alone for so long again. We were all the family that either of us had. Family should take care of family.

We were both lost in our own thoughts as we came around the big curve that brought us into the village of Newport. We were approaching the Wal-Mart when I looked in the rear-view mirror.

That's when I saw the Newport police cruiser behind us. I saw the red and blue lights start to flash just before I heard the siren. The officer behind the wheel was toggling the switch to the siren so that it chirped like an amplified bird being chased by the family tabby. We just passed the Welcome to Newport sign, and he must have been hiding behind, or around it. We were barely in the village. I pulled into the Wal-Mart parking lot and he stayed right on my tail, flashing and chirping all the way. I parked as far away from the store as I could so as to not attract too much attention. Still, everyone in the parking lot was watching. Officer Dan Dickenson stepped out of the car, and after adjusting his hat and gun belt, he took a quick look in the rearview mirror and walked slowly up to my window.

"Don't you believe in stopping when the police are behind you, Maxwell?" I thought that to be a silly question as I was stopped here, in the parking lot. Several smartass comments came to mind, and at that moment, I decided that I really didn't like this guy Dickenson.

"I thought it would be safer in the parking lot." I tried not to let my irritation show. I wanted to know why he pulled us over, but I waited him out.

"May I see your license and registration please?" His tone suggested that he was used to being obeyed. I could have sworn that he was watching himself in the reflection of the back window.

"How about you tell us why you stopped us." I sat quietly making no movement towards giving him the papers that he asked for.

"License and registration." This was not a polite question.

"As soon as you tell us why we are here."

"Alright smartass. We can do it the hard way. Out of the car." I started to get out of the car, and he grabbed me and pulled me out. He pushed me up against the car and in true cop fashion began to pat me down. I am not sure what he was looking for, but all he found was my phone, my wallet, and a folded church bulletin from the morning spent in Lockport. He put them all on the hood of the car. When he turned me around my fist was balled up, cocked and ready. He looked into my eyes daring me. He put one hand on the holster for his gun. He was smiling.

"Danny Dickenson, what on earth are you doing?" Aunt Liz had gotten out of the other side of the car. Her face was red. I knew too well that angry look. "You let him go."

"Ms. Dean, I didn't know you were in the car." His expression changed. I couldn't read it. Surprise for sure, but something else. Fear?

"Now, how in the heck could you not know. Can't you see?"

"Yes'm I can see." Dickenson's whole demeanor changed. It was like Aunt Liz's appearance on the scene let all the wind out of his sails. He was looking like that eighth grader that I encountered on my first stop to the police station. She was chastising the grown policeman like he was a kid who got caught with his hand in the cookie jar.

"Now Danny, what's the problem?"

"Ma'am, there has been some suspicious activity around town and this car fit the description of the vehicle."

"Don't you know this is my car?"

"Well, yes ma'am, I know it's your car."

"And you thought that maybe I was cruising around town causing this suspicious activity?"

"No, Ma'am." I could see his neck begin to flush red and watched as it crept up into his face.

"What did you think when you saw my car?"

"I didn't know it was your car Ms. Dean. I thought..."

"You thought that maybe my nephew, the famous author, was raising cane in your village? He decided to forgo his reputation for a little Sunday morning mischief?"

"No...yes. . . well..." He started stammering, and I could not help but smile. He saw me, and his look alone threatened to kill.

"Well, which is it?" Aunt Liz was in control, and I knew that the only way out now was for Dickenson to back down. I didn't believe his story about the car, and neither did Aunt Liz.

"I . . . uh... well... I must have been mistaken..." He tried to regain his composure. His eyes were still angry, and still focused on me. He turned and looked towards Aunt Liz. He took a deep breath. "Yes, I was clearly mistaken. I apologize Ms. Dean. Please continue on your way." Aunt Liz shook her head from side to side and he looked down as she got in the car.

"I will be watching you, pal," he said as I stepped in front of him to get back into the car. He moved to within two inches of my face and stared into my eyes. "This ain't over."

"You're right, pal, it ain't," I replied. "The way I see it you pulled us over for no reason and then assaulted me for no reason. Chief Munger's not gonna be too happy when he hears about this."

"I had a reason," he returned. The red in his face grew again. He spat on the ground next to my shoe. He spun around and walked back to his car. He was walking a lot faster than when he got out. I noticed that he not only looked like Barney Fife, but when he was angry, he walked like him too. He turned the lights out and spun the car around. Tires squealed as he pulled out of the parking lot and disappeared. I wasn't quite sure what we were into here, what exactly we had to finish, but I did know that it wasn't over. I wondered what our next meeting would be like.

"He was in my Sunday school class," Aunt Liz said as I got back in the car. I just looked at her. "Danny, he was in my class when I taught a few years back. He was never the sharpest stick in the pile." I had to laugh, and when I did, so did she. Until she remembered where we were going. Suddenly she stopped. And the tears began again.

TWENTY-THREE

For the second time in a week, I pulled into the driveway of someone who had died. Man, they were dropping like flies. A Newport police cruiser was parked on the street, and I saw Jack Munger leaning against it talking on his cell phone. My previously unanswered question about how Betty died resurfaced, and I wondered if Munger would be here if it wasn't foul play. If Betty was murdered, this was big. Treats had died by a blow to the head. When the big city news people got wind of another suspicious death, they would be all over this. Like ants to a picnic, it was only a matter of time before the big city TV trucks would arrive. Complete with portable satellite dishes they would scour the streets of Newport searching for the optimal broadcast location. Men and women, all perfectly coiffed and clothed and made up, standing in front of the station logo, cameras rolling, spilling the sordid details, whether true or not, hoping that the misfortunes of others would advance their careers.

The situation was the same, but the houses were very different. Old man Treats lived in an old Victorian built after the civil war. It was large and flamboyantly designed with a flamboyant history to match. Clover Heights was a classic model of that post-war twentieth century phenomenon known as a subdivision. A long, tree-lined, road entered into the tract and then circled around back on itself. All of the houses were either split-level or ranch style, and were all either black, white or gray. They fulfilled the unexplainable post-modern American's need to live exactly like their neighbor. The invention of television, and the barrage of constant advertising that it brings, has dumbed-down the American dream. Instead of creating another generation of truly American individuals that strike out on their own to establish their individuality, carving their piece of the dream out of that experience, young couples strive only to be exactly like the 'Joneses.' Success is now measured as a two-car garage, a quarter acre lot that always needs mowing, pizza hut boxes, Wal-Mart bags and McDonald's wrappers in the garbage. We all want to wear the same shirt, use the same deodorant, brush with the same toothpaste, and prove that we are valid members of the tract by cooking the same exotic recipe, learned by watching the same cooking expert on the same brand big screen television, on the same gas grills. All saddled with the same hefty mortgage that ties both the husband and the wife to jobs they don't like but cannot change.

All around the country, these subdivisions sprang up after the war. They continue today, and the contractors have managed to hone the system down to a science. In order to maximize profit, they offer two, maybe three variations on a house design. All are painted white on the interior, every room, and on the outside, they offer a choice of three colors: white, grey, or light blue long-lasting, maintenance-free plastic. The new homeowner can choose outside these parameters, of course, but it will cost them. The contractors consider these changes to be extra over-and-above the original contract, and have them figured at two to three times their actual cost putting either a lot more money in their pockets, or more likely putting most attempts to individualize out if the price ranges of young couples looking to move into their first new home. This leaves houses that all look the same, driveways all in the same place, and yards all the same size. Carmakers have followed suit, so add in Fords, Toyotas, and Chevys that all look the same. At night, it is impossible to tell one house from another, one street from another, and many stories have surfaced about men returning from bowling night, of golf with the boys, walking into the wrong house and climbing into bed with their neighbors' wife, or husband.

Several houses in Clover Heights had a small pole at the end of the driveway with flags, or reflective markers designed to provide that small spark of individuality that would ensure that the residents didn't accidently pull into the wrong driveway. As we pulled into the Clintons, I noticed that someone had painted a white plastic jug bright orange and stuck it upside down on a pole at the end of their driveway. The orange had begun to peel. *No confusing their driveway with another*, I thought as we pulled in.

There were several cars in the driveway, some parked on the grass in the front yard. I pulled into the front yard, next to a red Toyota. Maybe it was a Ford or Chevy. Aunt Liz got out, and ran into the house. I took one step to follow her then turned and headed towards Jack.

He turned towards the house and snapped his cell phone shut as he saw me approach. "Son of a bitch, Maxwell, what the hell are you doing here?"

"I came to see you, Jack." I was in a sour mood, and his attitude didn't help. "I missed you." I wanted to agitate the big guy. I wanted to poke at the bear with a stick. Dickenson's antics set me off, and I wanted some payback. "I missed your smiling face."

"Bullshit. Now, I'm only gonna ask one more time." He was looking at me with hard cop eyes. With all cops, everyone is guilty until proven innocent. The good ones don't believe in coincidence and now there were two prominent members of his community dead, a third if you count the funeral that Aunt Liz was at the day I arrived. I could see that Munger was trying to figure it all out, looking for common threads, and I could guess that he was thinking that these deaths occurred at the same time as I arrived, and I was at the scene with at least two. The good ones will work it over in their head, pursuing ideas, fed by leads and evidence, figure out who might have done it, and then try to bust their theory. Pick at it until it either proves to be true or unravels into a pile of impossibility on the floor. Once a theory is busted, the good ones will leave it alone and go to the next one. I was becoming a common thread. For Jack, the simplest answer was probably the right answer.

"You know why I'm here. Aunt Liz is a good friend. I brought her here." I was not willing to play nice.

"Um-hum." He pulled a small notebook out of his shirt

pocket. "It seems like since you get here, people are dying. It seems like every time someone dies you show up. Maybe you are returning to the scene? Maybe to check out your handiwork? Maybe you should just tell me where you were this morning?"

"Maybe it is none of your business." Still poking.

"You know, I'm in no mood for this shit. Maybe I should just arrest you now. Maybe you would like to sit in the can for a while. Maybe overnight. Call it attitude adjustment. Maybe you wanna tell me and the state guys all at once." I held my arms out towards him, my hands clasped together.

"What the fuck are you doing?"

"Let's go," I said. We stared at each other for a full minute. Neither one of us blinked.

"Put your god-damn hands down. You look like an ass." I watched as he processed information. He shook his head. He turned towards the car. Considering me as a suspect wasn't working. Sure, I was around any of these deaths, but only on the perimeter. I had a clear alibi for Treats. I was somewhere this morning, and not afraid of his efforts to intimidate. He wanted it to be me, for some reason, but it wasn't adding up in his head. I wasn't a player in these events in any way. In that one moment, it was clear to both of us that I wasn't a suspect. Jack's attitude changed. He was one of the good ones. He let it go. "I don't understand what the hell's going on."

"What happened here?"

"911 got a call about 9:30. It was George Clinton. What he does is go out to the cemetery every morning about 7 and walks a couple of miles. He then stops at the Towner for coffee. On Sundays, he comes home from the cemetery in time to pick up Betty and take her to church. Then he goes for coffee. When he got home this morning, she was lying on the kitchen floor. Someone had cracked her in the head. Real hard. Blood everywhere."

"Like Treats?"

"Yeah."

"Could it be the same weapon?"

"I don't know. It could be. We still haven't found what hit Treats. We have him in Monroe County at the morgue. They have the facilities to do a proper workup. I guess we'll send her there too."

"What about Earle, has he been here today?"

"Nobody has seen him all weekend. He didn't show up at the church this morning. And, I have about a dozen messages to his phone. He should be here for George, if nothing else." It would have been funny in another circumstance, but I could actually see the light come on in Munger's head. "You don't think he has anything to do with any of this?"

It was at this point that mutual respect kicked in. Jack had taken me into his confidence with information about the two murders. I decided to do the same. "Jack, all I know is that maybe nobody else has seen him this weekend, but he was sitting on the dock outside my boat this morning. He was at the marina waiting for me. He looked like he was in control; he was dressed as if he was going to work. Asked me if I was coming. He told me he would see me there. The thing is, I think he threatened me. His exact words were, 'somebody is going to get hurt if I don't back off.'" Jack asked questions. He made me tell him everything about Earle's visit. We stood in the road, and I told him everything I knew. I told him about the conversation with

Johnny, the conclusion that we had arrived at: that the school was fake, and maybe Earle was fake. I told him of my intentions to bring all of this to him the next day along with the information that Kim found.

"All in all, Jack, if we go with the assumption that Earle is a fraud, then the whole thing is beginning to crumble. My arrival and interest in the whole thing have been like an unwitting catalyst. Maybe it was starting to fall apart already. Maybe Cathy Paine's death was not accidental. If so, then things were beginning to go bad for Earle. If things are going bad, he might be making some desperate decisions. Make the assumption that Treats and Clinton decided not to give anymore and were pushing for an investigation. That might make Earle very nervous."

Jack took all of this in. He was in a tough spot. He clearly didn't want to believe that Earle was involved, but his cop sense kicked in. I knew at that moment that he was not just a local uniform, handing out parking tickets and gobbling donuts all day. He had a cop mind, and although it was a little rusty, it was coming to the surface. At this point, it was all circumstantial, but everything we knew pointed to Earle.

"Ok, assume," he said. "That Treats and Clinton were pushing for an investigation. It still doesn't add up. If it is all falling apart, why not just leave town? Killing people only creates more of a mess. It seems to me that the smart play would be to bundle up whatever he has stashed away and skip. Slip out in the middle of the night. Why kill?"

This was the same question Johnny and I were asking. "That's the part that gets me, too. Maybe this little town is paying off in a big way. A couple of deaths would be a small price to pay if he could get away with it and keep the cash flowing. He has to believe that he would be the last person on the list for anyone to suspect." So, Betty didn't die naturally. "Jack, the day I arrived, Aunt Liz had just returned from a funeral. One of the Paine sisters. How did she die?" Jack was lost in thought and I had to ask the question again. "Jack?"

"That was the damnedest thing. She fell out of the hay loft of an old barn behind their house." He looked shocked. "Jesus Christ, Maxwell. What the hell are you trying to do? You trying to tell me that Earle did that one too?" He started walking in circles. "Son of a bitch. She's already in the ground."

"I'm not saying anything, Jack. But she was giving money to that school too, and her sister found out. They had a big fight about it. Maybe she confronted Earle."

"Shit," He walked over to his cruiser. "You're pushing this too far." He reached into the car and pulled out the radio mic. "I am going to have a car run by Earle's place out on Canal Road. I think I will bring him in and see what he has to say for himself." He called for an officer to drive by Earle's. "Ask that son of a bitch if he would like to come down to the station. Be goddamn nice, but don't you dare come back without him." I wondered where Dickenson was. "No, just put him in the conference room, and hold him till I get there. I gotta wait here for the goddamn state guys to show up."

I decided that I wasn't going to play games anymore and told Jack where we were this morning. It was easy enough to check out. Plus, I got the feeling that he was no longer looking at me as a suspect. But the main reason that I wanted to tell him was to be able to tell him about Dickenson and our encounter in the parking lot. "He really pissed off Aunt Liz. She put him in his place though. I wouldn't be surprised if she makes a formal compliant when she gets enough time to think about it."

"Jesus Christ, that dumb bastard," he said. "Don't worry about him; I'll take care of it. He is just pissed off because you been seeing that McDermott girl. He's been mumbling about it for the past couple of days, but I didn't think anything of it." Again, he made me go through every detail. "Your aunt is a tough old broad." I heard respect in his voice. He thought about it a little more. "Shit, he's my best officer. I been thinking about making him assistant chief. Now he goes and makes a bonehead move like this? Shit."

I started to make a comment about how he could run his department better, when the radio in his car squawked. He walked over and stuck his substantial frame through the window. He was there for a couple of minutes. "That was Bates, the guy I had run by Earle's place," he said. "He says no one is there, but there is no sign of anything funny either. There is a dog in the front yard, and the back door is unlocked. It looks like Earle is planning to return."

"Maybe he should wait there until he does."

"Already did that," he stopped. "Jesus Christ, Maxwell, this is not my first day on the job. He will stay there until Earle comes back or his shift is over. Then we'll put the night guy on it. The village don't like me to pay overtime."

We were standing in the road and were forced to move when a red Prius came up the street. I looked to see who was driving and noticed that it was Kim. The snarl-smile immediately came to my face as she waved. Munger took note. She pulled over to the side of the road in front of Munger's police cruiser. At the same time, I heard the powerful rumble of a large block motor speeding up. Someone stepped on the gas and hard. Behind Kim and closing fast was another Newport cruiser. He sped past, angling the car around the circle, but not before we all got a look at Dickenson behind the wheel. He looked straight ahead. As Kim was getting out of her car and walking towards us, Dickenson came back around the circle. Driving slower now, he went past Kim and waved. He took off when he saw the look on Munger's face. Not happy. Jack was mumbling under his breath as he pulled the little notebook out of his shirt pocket and wrote something down. He didn't say anything. I liked that. Work business is work business, and we didn't need to know. I had the feeling that Dickenson was in for a very unpleasant conversation. Real soon. I turned my attention to Kim. She was just saying hi to Jack Munger, when two unmarked black Crown Victoria's pulled into the Clinton's driveway. The state guys. Four men in suits got out of each car. We took that as our cue to leave, and Kim and I headed towards her Prius.

TWENTY-FOUR

We made small talk as we travelled across town. We went over the old bridge that spanned the river, and into the older section of town. She turned down the tree-lined street where the old mansions were and pulled into the parking lot in front of an old sandstone Victorian. The street was lined with about a dozen Victorian mansions converted into apartment buildings. Hers was the center one in a group of three red brick houses. Hers was the biggest, surrounded on three sides by a large sandstone porch.

We went into the house and up the stairs. Her apartment was on the second floor facing the river. It looked like there were two other apartments on the second floor, but they must have all been small. The hallway and doors were all painted white and showed little of the style that was so prevalent by the outside of the building. Kim unlocked the door and we went in. It was small and some rooms were clearly cut up to allow for the other apartments. Painted in warm colors, the trim features that matched the period of the house were still intact. It was a nice little place. The living room was clean, and everything looked to be in its place. It was decorated in feminine pinks and red. There was a small television on the far wall opposite of a large white couch. The couch looked well-worn and comfortable. Two oak end tables with lamps, and a small coffee table that matched were all the furniture in the room. It looked welcoming. I walked through the living room over to a door on the other side. I looked out the window. It opened out onto a large balcony that covered the first-floor porch and spanned the entire riverside of the house. It too, was split so that two apartments could have private balconies. Kim had several plants on the railing, and a small green plastic table and chairs.

"Nice place." I turned. Kim was standing right behind me. We were face to face. She kissed me. I kissed her back. Boy did that feel good. Our tongues were once again exploring each other's mouths and I pulled her shirt over her head. She hesitated, but only for a second. Clothes flew everywhere and soon we were on the white couch together naked. We kissed and fondled, and I rolled over on top of her. Insistence and need overruled the need for foreplay, and we moved together using both the passion of the moment and the memories of the other night to heighten the experience. We brought each other to the edge, and backed down, only to rise again. We did this a couple of times until we could not wait. The ensuing climax was huge, and the world narrowed down to the feeling in my loins and the expression of passion in Kim's eyes. This moment lasted forever then was too fast gone. We lay sweaty and satisfied, in each other's arms. Holding tight and snuggling. It was hard to tell which arms, which legs belonged to which torso. It didn't matter. Neither of us moved. We didn't want to break the spell. Kim spoke first.

"Wow, you are trouble, mister," she grabbed my face and looked into my eyes. In the background, the embers of our passion still smoldered. Her expression was earnest and serious. "I swear I am not usually like this. You have a way, Mr. Maxwell."

"Yeah well, you know. Big stud here. Looking to blow into town, tumbling all the young ladies before leaving a trail of broken hearts behind." We both laughed.

"You probably are, ya big jerk." She smiled and hit me in the bare shoulder. "All I know is that this is first for this old couch. Hell, it is a first for this whole room; at least since I have been its occupant." She untangled. "Not exactly how I planned this evening."

"So, you wanted to eat first?"

"Something like that." She blushed and started to pick up her clothes.

"Well why don't we start again?" I stood and kissed her. "How about a drink on the balcony?"

"You read my mind, sir." She was putting her shirt back on. "But if you don't put some clothes on you are going to spend the evening with the village cops in a cold cell instead of with the pretty girl." I agreed, and after a couple more kisses, I gave her a hard smack on her bare behind and gathered up my clothes. Soon we were dressed and standing in her kitchen. I was put in charge of the drinks and set about creating the perfect gin and tonic. She had a bottle of Seagram's gin, and a couple of bottles of Schweppes tonic. Two tall glasses. Lots of ice and a wedge of fresh lime. Perfect. Kim was busy with a tray of vegetables and dip. We left the kitchen together. Me carrying the drinks. Her with the tray of veggies and a bag of Kettle potato chips.

Kim held the door and we stepped out onto the balcony. The sun had moved into the perfect position and was shining right into the balcony warming the old brick walls. The wind was blowing from the north and was blocked by the partition that separated her balcony from the other apartment. She took a sip of her drink, declared it good and sat down. She looked happy. I looked out over the railing and the plants that covered it. The river was about 100 feet away at the other end of the lawn. Past that was an unobstructed view of the back of several buildings downtown. I speculated that they were not there when this balcony was built. The rest of the village was obscured by trees with the exception of the steeples of the old churches on the square, and a couple of water towers in the distance. With the sun shining and the trees all greening up for spring, the view was incredible. I stood transfixed.

"Arn, aren't you listening? I asked you a question"

"What?" the spell was broken. I turned and sat.

"Typical man," she laughed. "Gets what he wants, then ignores the girl." I laughed too. "What I said was, how is Aunt Liz?"

"I think she is ok. She is a strong woman. The hardest part about being away all these years, is that I am not sure how to read her. She is not the same woman that I left, and I am not the same man. I know that all this death has upset her. Those people were her friends. I know that Earle's actions have upset her too. The Liz Sanderson I knew would be right in the middle of the fight. But the Liz

Sanderson I knew wouldn't have let Earle start taking her money in the first place. She is at her best when there is a problem to solve, or someone to care for. With that in mind, she is doing well. She ran right over to the Treats' and made me leave Lockport so that she could rush right over to be with George Clinton. The police hadn't even finished their investigation yet. I hope that she didn't go into the kitchen." I finished my drink. "But the day that I returned, what I saw was an old, frail woman. She was in an old housecoat, and Earle was visiting. The old Liz would never have been caught like that. She seemed to be bouncing back until all of this craziness began with Treats and Clinton. I hope she isn't overwhelmed."

"I think your assessment of your aunt is pretty accurate. She has been in the library a lot and since your uncle died, Evie and I both have noticed a decline. She has become thinner, quieter, less willing to stop and chat. She and Evie used to talk often catching up on the local gossip." She stopped for a minute. She ate a baby carrot and looked over the river. I got the feeling that she wanted to say something. She looked directly into my eyes. "I want to say something. I think that we know each other well enough now." I couldn't argue with that. I just nodded. I wanted to hear what she was going to say. "I think that she was lonely. Sure, she had the church, and the community. All of which banded together to help her when your uncle died. But he was gone, and you were gone. She used to tell Evie that she couldn't understand what she did to drive you away. You should have come home."

"Ouch." She landed a direct hit. Aunt Liz was lonely. That made sense. I turned and looked out over the river. My eyes fixed on the water tower on the other side of town.

Hindsight is twenty-twenty they say, and as I looked back. Kim's statement made sense.

"She would be lonely," I said. "After Uncle Bud died, who was left? Me. Arn Maxwell. Great sportsman and writer. Liver of the high life. I was after the great fishing experience. Living life to the fullest. There was nothing for me in Salmon Flats. So, I thought. I should have been with her. Looking back, I can see that you are right. I should have flown from Haiti as soon as I found out. Instead, I took the coward's way out. Lost in my own grief and guilt, my own problems, I justified my absence, and rationalized my actions, my inaction, of the last five years as being right for both of us. But right for who? Only me." Selfish me. As I sat on that balcony, I realized that the real guiding precept of the last five years, and probably a few before, was that I began to believe the hype. I continued. "I was Arn Maxwell, famous writer. I had money. I had success. Readings…talk shows… radio interviews. I was in demand. I had an entourage of people working for me. Agents, financial advisors, an accountant. But as much as I had, I forgot about what I lost. I forgot the young boy walking the beach with his father and his uncle. Picking rocks for the entranceway of Uncle Bud's new house. Signing the bottoms in permanent marker for all eternity. I forgot how good it felt to be with family. The feeling of security and well-being. I forgot about friends. About gin and cigars behind the barn. I was Arn frickin Maxwell, goddamn it. I didn't need any of that. I had Cindy and a great life in Florida. That's where all the guilt came from, and the shame. That's why I could not face her. Returning home, returning to her, only after everything went sour. That felt like failure. My failure. It is clear now, that everything was going sour for both of us. She needed me. Aunt Liz and I were the only ones left. We should have been together. Needed to be together." Kim watched as I worked my way through her statement. She saw the sadness and regret in my eyes. Without speaking, she saw what I was going through. She understood. Without a word, she took me by the hand and led me to her bedroom.

TWENTY-FIVE

There is a moment in every relationship where love enters. It can come with a look, or a small gesture, a touch of the hand, perhaps a smile. A realization that this person's presence in your life means a whole lot more than it did even a few moments ago. It can happen the very first time two people meet, or after time getting to know one another. For us it was that simple gesture. Kim took me into her bedroom. She slowly removed my clothes. She pulled me down onto her bed, and for the second time this afternoon, we were naked. For the first time ever, we made love. The physical passion we felt for each other heightened by the emotional passion that was born by the simple act of understanding. We moved together. Synchronized in a new way that brought new sensations. Fueling the drive to please each other, and in pleasing be satisfied ourselves. Fueled by love.

We looked into each other's eyes and the rest of the world went away. Gone was Earle and his school. Gone was my selfishness. Gone were Aunt Liz, and the last five years of loneliness. Gone were Treats and Clinton, and Munger, and Dickenson. Gone was the broke, homeless man seeking to disappear. All that was left were those Key West eyes. Wide and full of emotion. At the same time, release filled every part of our conjoined being. Our eyes feasted on passion-filled faces and bodies that were seeking to be one. All circuits joined. I saw her in a new light, and understood her in a new way. I saw her as she saw me. I saw myself as she saw me. I felt good.

I resolved right then and there that if I never felt this way again, it would be ok. I had felt true, uncompromising, unconditional love. This day, this moment would be recorded in the big book. The scribe sharpening his quill, opening to a new parchment page: scratching the time, and the place. The way the girl smelled, and tasted, and felt as she snuggled, head resting on my bare chest. Spent, we lay together. Conversation changed from the here and now to the future. What would we do next week? When would we be able to sail around the lake? Maybe Evie would give her a couple of weeks off in July. Maybe I wouldn't go back to Florida.

We decided not to get dressed as we got up and walked to the kitchen. Kim had a pot roast in the Crockpot, and it smelled wonderful. As she stirred, I saw potatoes, onions, carrots, cloves of garlic. I fixed us each another gin and tonic and sat on a bar stool on the living room side of the kitchen counter. The bare wood seat was cold. She looked beautiful bustling around the kitchen naked. She reached into an upper cabinet and brought out a bottle of Leonard Oakes merlot and two glasses. I opened the wine and set it on the counter to breathe.

I mixed fresh drinks and set plates out on the counter. I ran to the bedroom where my clothes were and grabbed my phone. I decided to call Aunt Liz. I wanted to make sure she was ok. I walked back into the living room and sat back down. The wood was still cold. Kim was chopping romaine lettuce. She had piled red onions, baby carrots, celery, grape tomatoes, and a couple of boiled eggs on the counter and was building a salad. The phone rang, went to voicemail. I tried her home phone. No answer.

We got dressed before we ate. The sun had set, and the spring evening cooled down the apartment. Kim stated as she reached for the wine glasses that she was a little chilly, and not in the habit of running around her house naked. She wanted to have some clothes on. What if she spilled? I agreed. We both dressed. As we ate, we got to know each other better. We talked about our pasts, living in and around Newport. We noted similarities and differences given our age difference. We found that we knew a lot of the same people, but she kept referring to my friends as part of an older crowd. Of course, her friends were just little kids. We got a lot of mileage out of that. The laughter was comfortable and good. Playful teasing back and forth with no edge of malice. Just bantering. My heart lit up every time she smiled. As we finished, and I poured one last glass of wine, she started clearing the table. I tried Aunt Liz again. Again, no answer.

We cleared the dishes. The kitchen was really small, and we bustled around washing and putting ways the remains of our dinner. There was a lot of playful bumping and touching. I cannot remember the last time I had so much fun with a woman. Maybe it was like this when Cindy and I first started, but the tensions of the last few years changed all that and overwrote any memories that might have preceded. I silently hoped that she could find some happiness. I had. While we were doing the dishes, she asked me about Betty Clinton. I told her what Jack and I talked about. When I got to the part about my suspicions surrounding Earle, she just stared at me with an open mouth.

"Can't be," she said." He is a kind and gentle man. I cannot see him hurting a fly."

"I didn't realize you knew him that well."

"I don't, but it is a small town, and everybody knows everybody else, at least a little. He always seems a little distant when he comes in the library, but always polite. He just radiates the presence of someone who wouldn't commit any violence."

"Even if threatened?"

"I don't know about that. Maybe if he was threatened. But I agree with you and Jack. The smart move is to just run."

"Well, Jack promised to get to the bottom of it. He has a deputy out looking for him now. I told Jack that we would bring everything we knew to him tomorrow morning." I sat down on the couch.

"Don't get too comfortable mister." I just looked at her. "There are many eyes in this little neighborhood, and I am not about to let us become fodder for the Monday morning coffee crowd. Besides, tomorrow is a workday, and if the pretty girl doesn't get her 8 hours, she won't be a very pretty girl tomorrow." I didn't want to go. So, I grumbled my way back down the stairs and into the Prius. We hugged and kissed for about ten minutes in the marina parking lot before I finally sent her on her way.

"If you don't go now, I am going to drag you out the docks and lock you into the forward cabin. Never to be seen again." I tried to look menacing. She just laughed. I stood in the parking lot until I could not see her taillights. I felt good. Maybe it was the right thing to escape all the chaos of my Florida life. Maybe it was good to be home. I put my hands in my pockets and slowly walked back to Bella. Just maybe.

TWENTY-SIX

I unlocked Bella and went below. It was too cold to sit outside, so I sat at my galley table. I grabbed a beer and a cigar. I hit the power button on my laptop. Checked my email. Nothing. I opened the document that I started the other day. Not really a story, but thoughts about the whole Earle situation. Titled "Good or Bad." I re-read, made some changes and then started adding what had happened today. I stopped after an hour. It felt good to write. For the first time in a couple of years, words flowed. Like the old days, they flowed onto the page. Five pages of facts and suppositions. Five pages. It wasn't much, but after years of nothing. After not even being able to face the blank page, the blinking cursor taunting me, and accusing me of being a has-been. Or maybe a never-was. These five pages felt great. I re-read them. Not great prose, but it felt right. The facts were there, and they supported the suppositions and conclusions. I sat back. I was riding high. I was basking in post-coital bliss, fueled and prolonged by the buzz that I had started with the first gin and tonic at Kim's, and continued as I finished the last of the beer in front of me. This all blended with feelings of love that both surprised me and felt right at the same time. I thought of calling her. I reached for the phone and remembered that she wanted to get some sleep. I set it down and grabbed another beer. I re-read what I wrote. It was good. I wondered if Hemmingway wrote this way and was inspired after an afternoon out on the boat, or at Sloppy Joes. Finally feeling motivated and staggering home to write. Did his lifestyle destroy him, as critics believe, or was it the muse that allowed him to achieve greatness? I don't know, I never wrote in this condition before, but as I watched the thin curls of smoke rise from my cigar, culminating in the foggy cloud on my ceiling, I thought that I would always get drunk and have sex before I wrote from now on. What a tough way to make a living. I wrapped up my narrative with a final conclusion:

It is now overwhelmingly clear that the school in Africa never existed. No evidence has been found, and none provided by Reverend T. Whitman Earle. In this matter he has committed fraud, taking full advantage of his position to deceive people looking to him for guidance. As a man of the cloth, their default reaction was to trust him. Is he though? It will require further investigation into his background to determine for sure, but evidence now points to that being untrue also. It is my opinion that his credentials have been falsified. Evidence and conclusions in this document also point to him being the one that killed Treats, and Betty Clinton. And maybe Cathy Paine. My insertion into the mix has acted as a catalyst, causing an already unstable situation to crumble completely. This has led to Earle's need to destroy anyone in the way. Two for sure, (Treats and Clinton) and one maybe (Paine). All were questioning his actions, all were stalling, all wanted proof of the school. Proof that he could not provide. All had to be removed. The one question that has to be asked, and answered, is on everyone's mind. If he is a conman and if he came to Newport with the intention of defrauding, and if it was starting to go bad, why didn't he just take the money and run?

I closed the file and shut down the computer. I had another beer while I finished my cigar. My thoughts were on Kim, and writing, and Newport, the whole mess, and my life, and writing, and reasons to stay, and reasons to go back to Florida, and writing. I decided I had better go to bed. I staggered as I stood up and grabbed the counter to hold me up. I was drunker than I thought. I stumbled into bed, the room spinning. As my head hit the pillow, and sleep encroached, I had two thoughts. If Hemmingway was writing like this, he was a better man than me. Also, would I look at what I wrote in the morning and still like it? The room stopped spinning for a moment, and I went to sleep.

TWENTY-SEVEN

Monday morning was cold, but the sun was shining through the porthole windows when I woke up. I rolled over under the blankets and decided that I would need to get a heater if I was going to continue living on the boat. I looked at the alarm clock mounted on the headboard. 9:45. I put on an old sweater and jeans and padded into the galley for a cup of coffee. With just a touch of half-and-half, the hot brew warmed my insides and cleared my head at the same time. Almost ten o'clock. Kim would be hard at work. I thought of sending her a text. I got my phone but couldn't think of anything clever to say. Writer's block on a text. Bad news. Instead of texting Kim, I decided to try Aunt Liz. I was a little concerned that she didn't answer last night, but it was a long day. Maybe she was just tired. Maybe she just went home and went to bed. I dialed her home phone; she should be up and about by now. No answer. I tried her cell, voicemail. Hmmmm. I decided to go over and make sure she was ok.

I scrambled up some eggs and ate them out of the pan, standing over the sink. I filled my coffee cup, and then realizing that there was no way to drink it in Ol' Betsy, I took two big gulps and left the cup on the counter. I slipped into a pair of old boat shoes and with the keys in hand, headed towards the parking lot. I stopped in my tracks on the other side of the marina store. Ol' Betsy was not there. The spot by the dumpster was empty. It took a couple of minutes of searching the cloudy mind recesses to remember that I left the truck in Aunt Liz's driveway. I should have let Kim drop me over there last night. I debated trying to find a ride and decided it would be easier just to walk. By the time I crossed the bridge, I found my stride, and my head was beginning to clear. When I turned onto the lake road heading towards Aunt Liz' house, I was whistling.

When Aunt Liz' house came into view, I could see Ol' Betsy parked in the driveway. Everything else was quiet. Even the neighbors were inside or away. Probably off to work, most of them. As I approached the driveway, I wondered if Aunt Liz would have any more of those muffins that we had the other day. I looked in the window of the garage. Her car was there. I walked up the porch and looked in the window to the foyer. I didn't see her. I knocked. No response. I tried the door; it was unlocked. I walked in. "Aunt Liz? It's Arn." In the kitchen, everything was in place except for a small dish, spoon, and coffee cup that were in the sink. Leftover from breakfast. I called again. No answer. I walked through the house. Nothing. I walked out onto the porch. The table and a couple of chairs were flipped over. The glass top of the table was cracked, lying flat on the floor. The lamp that was on the side table was on the floor broken. There was a small puddle of almost dried blood on the carpet. I lost it. I ran from room to room yelling for Aunt Liz.

I ran outside. I looked over the break wall to the beach. I looked in the garage, around, in, and under her car. I popped the trunk. Nothing. I could feel the panic rising. I ran out of the garage. I even looked under the back porch. I stood in the driveway. I didn't know what to do. I couldn't think. I grabbed my phone and started to call Munger. Before I hit send, I remembered that this was not his jurisdiction. I stopped in my tracks. Think, Maxwell, get control. I was going to have to go inside to look up the sheriff's phone number. I walked around the other side of the truck, headed towards the back door. For the first time, I saw two tracks in the gravel driveway. Parallel almost identical grooves. Someone else had been there and had left in a hurry. Most likely with Aunt Liz.

TWENTY-EIGHT

That son of a bitch. That fuckin' Earle. This time he got Aunt Liz. This time he took her instead of killing her. Maybe she was still alive. I ran around the truck, pulling the keys and phone out of my pocket. I started the truck and backed out. I left almost identical groves in the driveway. The tires squealed at every stop sign until I finally turned on the road where Earle's house was. About five miles to go. I tried Munger. This was definitely in his jurisdiction. Voicemail. I left a long and detailed message, all at the top of my lungs. Panic was beginning to set in. Travelling at almost 80, the old truck was shaking. The heavy-duty tires rumbled on the asphalt. Smoke started coming out of the back of the truck, and I silently apologized to the old girl, and to young Dale Davis working to rebuild her. I was bouncing over the rough, country road, holding on to the steering wheel with both hands to keep from bouncing off the seat and losing control. I only slowed a little as I charged up the hill to the old single lane bridge that went over the canal. I hoped that no one was on the other side. As the back tires hit the steel deck of the bridge, they lost traction, and the back of the box hit the side of the bridge. I looked in the rearview mirror in time to see the box crumple, and the back-bumper bounce twice on the steel, coming to rest in the middle of the road. More apologies, but I didn't slow down. Earle's house was on the other side of the bridge. I could see the roofline. I stepped on the gas.

Sliding almost sideways, I stopped the truck across the street from Earle's house. His Cadillac was pulled up close to the carriage house next to the main house, and a Newport police cruiser was parked at an angle behind it. Good. Munger was already here. I looked across the expanse of the front lawn. To my right was an old cobblestone farmhouse. The carriage house sat in the middle of the scene, and to the left nestled in a grove of pine trees was a square screened-in gazebo. Some of the screens were ripped and falling out. Behind the house, I could see part of an outbuilding that looked like an old stone barn. It was silent except for the birds in the trees. No sign of Earle, or Munger, or Aunt Liz. I crossed the road and up the driveway. I walked past the cars and peered into carriage house. It took a couple of seconds for my eyes to adjust to the dark, but everything was still. I walked over to the house. The side door was open. I slipped in. I didn't want to surprise anybody. I looked around the house. There wasn't any sign of activity, or violence. With more confidence, I walked back out into the yard. The only place left to look was in the stone barn. I headed that way.

I walked around the south side of the barn. The large wooden barn doors were on the back of the barn. They were open and hanging on an old iron track that stuck out past the wall. I kept close to the barn, and had to walk around an old gasoline tank, piped to a hand crank pump. The tank was rusted, and the pump handle looked like it hadn't turned in years. The gauge was stuck between 0000, and 9999. The tank was rusty, and when I passed it, I wondered if there was any gas in it. I moved around the barn doors. They were both open. There was a large window on the other side of the barn. I could see inside. I surveyed the room.

The walls of the barn were post and beam framework with stone and mortar filling in, creating both the interior and exterior walls. Hooks and rings hung from the vertical beams. A couple had old farm tools hanging from them. One, a shovel. Around the perimeter of the barn were a dozen wooden four-by-four posts. They were driven into the dirt floor about a foot from the wall, and four feet apart. They looked to be about six feet tall. In the back, tied to one of the posts sat Reverend Earle. His hands were tied behind his back. His face was covered in dried blood and swollen. There was a rope around his neck, and around the pole holding him up. It was tied tight, and the rope dug into his skin. He looked like he was listening attentively to some far-off sermon. His lifeless eyes looked through me. Staring. He was dead. It was also clear that his last few hours on this earth were not pleasant.

To his right, tied to the next post, sat Aunt Liz. Her hands were tied behind her back, and a rope was around her neck also. It did not dig into her skin. I ran over to her. The whole left side of her face was covered in blood from a large wound on her head. She was still. She sat motionless, with her eyes closed. I knelt beside her. I put my hand on her shoulder. She was wearing the same dress that she had on yesterday. The cloth was wet. When I pulled my hand away it was red. I looked her over. The knot on her head had quit bleeding, but it looked bad. The area around the cut was depressed. Like a melon after being hit with a baseball bat. Something had hit her hard. I checked her pulse. She let out a soft moan at my touch. The sound startled me and I jumped back, falling on my back in the middle of the barn. I stood up. She didn't move again.

Holy shit. I could feel the panic rising again. I wanted to scream. I wanted to run. I walked around in circles, trying to get a grip on the situation. Earle was dead; that was pretty clear. And, someone had hit Aunt Liz, and kidnapped her, and brought her to Earle's house. Nothing made sense. I heard a young girl crying. I looked around and realized that it was me. The edges were getting fuzzy, I was losing focus. I didn't know what to do. I kept walking around in circles. I jumped up and down a couple times and started to scream when it hit me. I had to get her some help.

I reached in my pocket for my phone. It wasn't there. More circles. Where the hell was it? After the fourth time around, I remembered that after trying to get Munger, I tossed it on the front seat of the truck. Speaking of Munger, where the hell was he anyway? I had to go out and get it. I took a deep breath. I had to get it together if I was going to help Aunt Liz. Ok, Maxwell. Time to be man. Make sure she's still alive then go out to the truck and call 911. Now. I checked her pulse again. It was still thumping steadily. I looked her in the eye. The look on her face seemed to be saying, 'Hurry Arn! I don't have much time.'

"Hold On, Aunt Liz," I said out loud. "I'll be right back."

I jumped up and ran out of the barn. I heard a noise behind me, instinctively I reacted to the movement behind me and started to duck. I saw a bright white light as pain exploded inside my head. My poor attempt to get out of the way, and the momentum of the blow catapulted me forward, and I rolled twice stopping in front of the old gas tank. I looked to see what hit me. Blood was running into my eyes, and I couldn't see anything. The world began to close around me. As I passed out, I saw a bee fly out of the nozzle of the old pump.

TWENTY-NINE

Like being unexpectedly roused from a sound sleep, I opened my eyes and could not remember where I was. Almost instantly, the pain in my head came alive, and I tried to touch the spot that hurt. I couldn't move my hands. As I turned my head to find out what was wrong with my hands, something was scratching my throat, limiting movement. I couldn't breathe. I tried to clear my head. The wires reconnected. The lenses began to re-focus. The picture was beginning to take shape. I was sitting on the dirt floor of the old barn, leaning against a pole, hands tied behind my back. There was a rope around my neck. The last memory was of walking out of the barn to get my phone. I never saw what hit me. I turned as far as I could and could see Aunt Liz and Earle. I tried to move. My hands were taped together. They hurt. The lack of circulation was making them tingle. The pain helped clear my head, and I assessed the situation. The tape had to be the same gray duct tape that bound the other two. The rope too. Whoever did this must have been outside the barn. Boy, I walked into that one. I tried to pull the tape apart until my shoulders hurt. It didn't budge. I tried again, until ligaments started to pop in my shoulders, almost screaming with the effort. I stopped. I had to get out of this. I had to help Aunt Liz. She was leaning forward. All of her upper body weight was being held up by the rope around her neck. Her face was beginning to turn blue. I struggled but found that any attempt to move only increased the resistance around my throat. I sat back coughing. Tried to catch my breath. I had to get in touch with Munger. I had to get to my phone. I rested. Tried to come up with a plan. I could feel blood running down my left hand. I felt the pole and found a sharp edge. Just above the tape, there was a sliver of wood sticking out. I must have dislodged it a little with my actions. I tried to pick at the tape. Soon I found that if I tensed up, I could position my hands so that I could poke holes in the tape. The only problem was that this required a full body strain, and I could only poke a couple of holes before the rope stopped my breathing and I had to stop. After a couple of tries, I got so that I didn't poke myself every time and the process didn't hurt as much. I was just getting started when I heard whistling outside the barn.

The whistling was coming closer. I poked two more holes and slumped to the floor, faking unconsciousness. I tried to identify the tune. I thought it was one from my childhood, but he was a little flat and I couldn't pull up the right memory. He walked around the corner. With his police hat set on the back of his head, and his uniform, neatly pressed, and shoes, and belt spit-shined, he looked more like the fabled Mayberry deputy than ever. Dan

Dickenson looked at me and quit whistling. Trying to tell if I was alive or dead. In his hands was a club. I hoped that my eyes still looked closed as I watched him. At first, I thought it was a baseball bat, but as he came closer, I could see Oscar standing on the top of a short Iron pole. So, that was why there were only four on one side of Treats' garden. He walked slowly into the room, towards Aunt Liz. He leaned the weapon against the wall and knelt to touch her throat, feeling for a pulse. He nodded and looked around her back. He checked the tape. Satisfied he walked over to Earle.

"No need to check you, now, is there, Reverend?" he said. "You just aren't going anywhere." He chuckled and patted Earle on the head. Instinctively he still looked behind Earle to make sure that the tape was secure. He turned to me. I was slack, and my eyes were mostly closed. I closed them as he neared. I didn't want him to check my hands. "How 'bout you, Mr. Maxwell? How are you today?" He put two fingers on my neck. "Well, that little bump on the head didn't kill you, did it?" He walked back to get his club. He stopped and turned around. I could feel his breath on my face. When I sensed that he was close, I popped my eyes open. At the same time, I yelled at the top of my lungs, and strained against the rope. The effect was to scare, and it worked. Dickenson jumped back and fell to the ground. He rolled to his right and was on his feet in one motion. He was fast. He walked over to me. He slapped me.

"You scared the shit out of me," he said. He slapped me again. "You must have a really hard head." Adrenalin was pumping, I wanted to jump this guy and beat the crap out of him. I strained against the restraints. He was standing in front of me. I looked him in the eye while I poked a couple more holes in the tape. Spent, and breathing hard, I slumped back to the floor. He smiled and patted me on the head. "No problem." He slapped me a third time. That one hurt. He started whistling again. Still couldn't make out the song. Still flat.

"Dickenson, what the hell is going on here? Where is Munger?"

"Munger? That fat bastard is probably sittin' in front of a plate of donuts at the Towner. He hasn't got a clue."

"He's not the only one. What the hell is going on here? Who the hell killed Earle? He killed all those others. Who killed him? How did Aunt Liz get here? Did you hurt her? Why would you do that?"

"You know, you are really not that smart. It's no wonder you lost it all. You had money, fame, a hot wife. Now you got shit. Just a leaky old boat." He slapped me again. Again, I strained to get loose. Two more holes in the tape before I stopped. I could feel it starting to give.

"Dickenson, what the fuck. You got him now. Call Munger. He can get help for Aunt Liz. He can get us out of here." I was staring him down. As a kid, I spent hours reading superman comics on the front porch on lazy summer afternoons. I tried to figure out how he could direct heat from his eyes, enough to melt steel. I always imagined that it was anger that got that fire going, because his expression was the same one that I was using right now. If I had any superpowers at all, I would be burning a hole right though Dickenson's eyes.

"Yeah. No, I don't think so. See you got it all wrong." He sat cross-legged in front of me. We were eye to eye. I was still trying to conjure up that heat beam. "You got it all wrong, man. Earle couldn't hurt a fly."

"Then who. . .?" The light went on. My face registered my shock.

"There you go," he laughed. "You know, you really aren't too bright. I still don't see what she sees in you. Doesn't matter now."

"So, you killed all those people?"

"Yeah. I probably shouldn't have, huh? The first one was by accident. That Paine woman was arguing with me, she got in my face and I pushed her. I didn't know that the door was unlocked. She fell out the second floor of the barn. It was listed as an accident, but then I was the one that filled out the report."

"But why?"

"Money. What else is there? I need to get out of this piece of shit town, and I need money."

"You killed Earle for money? What about the rest?"

I killed them all for money, dumbass." He did a fairly good imitation of Jack Munger. "Actually, it was because they wanted to stop giving money. Except Old Liz there. I did that to piss you off. Oh, and you. I am gonna do that because I don't like you. And Kimmy. Gonna get her next. That fuckin whore." He stood and walked over to Earle. "This son of a bitch. Started to get all noble on me too. He wanted to stop. To run. He was holding out. I brought him out here and tied him up. It took me all morning yesterday to get him to tell me where he hid the money. I was surprised at how much he could take. Used to strain just like you do. I just kept hittin' him. Finally, he broke. At the end, he was blubberin' and prayin'. There was a hundred thousand in his basement, in an old cistern. That's not even half of it, but the dumb bastard died before I could get the rest. That last pop on the head was too much, I guess. I was looking for the rest when I heard you hit the bridge. That was smooth; way to sneak up on the situation. I guess I'm gonna hafta' settle for that hundred grand. I can't find any more, and time is running out. I blame you for all of this, Maxwell. If you hadn't stuck your nose where it doesn't belong, all these people would still be alive, they would have given me all their money, and I would be long gone."

"But it was Earle defrauding everyone. How did you get into this?" He slapped me again. I strained against the rope. More holes in the tape. I was going to beat him to death. He timed the next slap so that he hit me just before my head rested on the pole. I saw stars as the back of my head bounced off the pole.

"You know, this is just how I did with the good reverend over there. I wonder if you can take as much as him. Do you think you are as tough as a preacher man?" He slapped me again. I was fading in and out. I fought to stay conscious.

THIRTY

Dickenson walked to the other side of the barn. He grabbed an old wooden chair and brought it back to face me. He sat down. He pulled a crumpled pack of Camels from his shirt pocket and lit one. He was watching me like a hawk. I struggled to clear my head. I shook violently, trying to keep from passing out. That last one was bad. If he kept that up, I was a goner. He just sat there, staring, smoking.

I had to get loose. Figure out a way to overpower him so that I could get to Aunt Liz. I wasn't sure if I could. My hands were hurting, and my legs had fallen asleep. It hurt to move them. I wasn't sure if I could move them even if I did get free. My head was cloudy. We stared at each other. I tried to burn a hole in his skull again. It didn't work. I pulled on the tape. I felt it give. I heard it tear and stopped. My hands were coming loose, but I didn't want him to know that. I needed a distraction. I decided to wait.

He ground the cigarette into the dirt floor and started

talking. "That sorry son of a bitch," he began. "Everyone was glad to see him come to town. He was smart, good looking, and started right away to make an impact. Within weeks, he had the village eating out of his hand. After he was here about six months, we received a missing person's report. I saw a Tom Earle on the list. I did a little checking on my own, figured it might be the same guy, and found out that Tom Earle was reported missing from a town in Ohio. I decided to confront him and find out what was going on." He stood up and walked over to the wall. He picked up the garden post that looked like Oscar and walked over to Earle's body. He tapped him on the head, not softly. It made a sickening sound. Kind of like hitting a rotten watermelon. Earle's body rolled with the blow. "Sorry son of a bitch." Dickenson sat back down in front of me and leaned forward with both hands on the post. "I caught him at the church one afternoon. He and I were the only ones there. I questioned him. At first, he denied everything. I 'persuaded' him to tell me. You might say I put the fear of God in him."

He slapped the post and laughed. "I threatened to call Ohio. Eventually he talked.

Apparently, he got involved with a young female member of his church. They spent more and more time together. It all came to head one night at the church, and he came close to consummating that relationship. He got scared. He tried to stop it. The scene ended badly, and the girl threatened to tell her parents that they did, even though they didn't. She was under-age. Earle panicked. He had complete access to an account they created to start a new school in Africa. He cleaned that out and ran. He changed his looks a little, reworked his resume, started calling himself T. Whitman instead of Tom, and turned up here in Newport. He told me the whole story. By the time he finished, he was a broken man. He was crying and ready to turn himself in. He was fully expecting me to arrest him. I didn't want to arrest him; I had other ideas. He would do anything for me so that wouldn't happen. While I was listening to him tell his sorry story, I hatched a plan. Create a school fundraiser here in Newport. Milk as much money as I could out the town and finally get out of here. Earle was more than willing to cooperate if it kept him out of jail. I even sweetened the pot by promising to let him keep some of the money. I figured I could screw him out of that later. It was working perfectly too. I swear the man has a gift for getting money out of these tight old bastards. Had an honest to God gift, stupid fuck."

"So, this is about money?"

"No, the money is only a bonus. There is a lot of money in this shithole little town. Especially in that Presbyterian crowd. I have been thinking about it for years, and finally had a way to get me some."

"So, what then?"

"I'm dyin' in this piece of shit job, in this piece of shit town. Ten years I been working swing shifts. Ten years married to that fat old bitch. Handling drunks at two in the morning. All wanting to fight or throwing up in the back of the squad car. Then home to her and those screaming brats. Ten years I played the game. Looking the other way when the mayor wrecked his car. Helping the town council's kids when they got in a jam. All for what? So that self-righteous prick McCabe could appoint Munger over me. No this isn't about money. It is about getting even." He stomped out the cigarette. "Although I do like money. I wish I could stay and find the rest, but I think I am gonna need to leave today. I may have done all I can around here."

"So why kill them. Why not just get the money from Earle and run?"

"That's what I was gonna do. Everything was beginning to go sour. I coulda' got away with killing to Paine woman. Hell, I did get away with it. But I wanted to get the payment that that old bastard Treats was supposed to make. It was for about twenty Gs. That would have made sure I had enough. He decided not to give it to Earle. He was waiting to find out what you dug up. I went to his house to persuade him to change his mind, and he told me that it was none of my business. He threw me out. That fucker. Threw me out. He found out whose business it was when I clocked him with that ugly garden thing. Betty Clinton was different. She figured out, somehow, that I was behind it all. She is either smarter than the rest of you, or that coward, Earle, told her. I had the garden post in the trunk of my cruiser. She went down with one swing." He smiled. He had a story to tell, and he was proud of it. I wanted to slap that smug look off his face.

"But why Aunt Liz?"

"You saw the way she treated me yesterday. She has been talking down to me forever. She was good friends with my parents. She has never stopped treating me like their ten-year-old son. I figured what the heck, what's one more? She got hysterical when I brought her in here and she saw Earle. I had to hit her to shut her up. Besides, I knew it would piss you off. When I saw you leave with Kim, I decided I needed to do something. I followed her home and took her just after she got in the house. I figured someone would find them here long after I was gone. I didn't expect that you would actually come blundering into all this. Now they will find you too. That's like icing on the cake."

"You are a sick man, Dickenson. You gotta stop this now."

"Too late for that, my friend."

"I'll tell you what. If it's money you want, I'll give you twenty grand to let me go."

"First of all, I don't believe you got twenty grand."

"Let me go. I gotta help Aunt Liz. There's twenty grand stashed on my boat."

"What? Oh. Let you go?" He started to laugh. "Yeah, no, I don't think so. You are going to die here. But I like the idea of the boat. I'll take the boat and the money. You won't need them. That might be a better escape route than I planned." He was thinking. He started walking back and forth in front of me, talking to himself. "Take the boat, and the twenty grand. He won't need it anymore. Cross the lake, and into a small harbor. No better yet, an empty bay, and sink her. Maybe I'll take that little slut Kimmy with me too, for the ride. Yeah. Sink her with the boat." He was smiling. Proud of himself again. He looked at me. "How's that sound, Maxwell? Your boat, your money, your girl. You can die knowing how badly I am going to abuse her. And, in your bed. This just keeps getting better and better. Yeah. And I wouldn't worry about Aunt Liz, it's too late for her anyway." He walked over to Aunt Liz. He crouched down so that he could be eye level with her. When he was about two inches from her face he spoke, "You're already gone aren't you, you old bitch." As he said that her eyes popped open, and she screamed. She was straining against the rope with every ounce of energy she had left. I could see the veins popping out of her neck. Dickenson yelped and fell backwards in shock. Aunt Liz was still alive and pulled the ultimate surprise.

THIRTY-ONE

Aunt Liz fell silent again. I jumped on the opportunity. Dickenson was rolling on the floor trying to regain his composure. The perfect distraction. I ripped the tape and my hands came apart. I pulled at the rope around my neck and it came loose. I jumped up and my legs gave way. I stumbled forward, falling towards Dickenson. I tackled him just as he was beginning to stand up. He was reaching for his gun. We both tumbled across the barn floor. I hopped up, and on legs that felt like wooden twigs, ran for the open door. They were tingling, starting to return to life. Every step was painful but getting stronger. I had to get to the truck and my phone. It was about two hundred yards away, in the wide-open yard of Earle's house. My plan was to run real fast. Get behind the truck, call Munger and hold out until he got there. The first part of the plan was to be way ahead of him. Getting to the truck before he could get a hold of the gun and finish me off. I felt the first shot before I heard it. It chunked solidly into the old wooden doorframe spraying me with splinters. Dickenson was on one knee with the gun in both hands. He looked extremely competent, and I felt extremely lucky as I rounded the barn and headed into the orchard. I heard a second shot go off but didn't hear it hit anything. I ran into the orchard, heading for the canal bank, zigzagging around apple trees, trying to make it hard for Dickenson to draw a bead. Four more shots rang out, but nowhere near me. I got to the edge of the orchard and there was a large ditch filled with thick bushes between me and the canal. I couldn't see the bottom of the ditch and couldn't find a way through. Dickenson came out of the barn and was walking my way. I looked back and saw him getting closer. I hid under an old apple tree. He was walking directly towards my apple tree and reloading his pistol. I jumped into the ditch. I crab-crawled along the edge, keeping low so that he couldn't see me moving, but I could not find a way through the brush. I skirted lengthways down the bank, moving farther away from the barn and the truck, stopping every few feet to locate Dickenson. He was weaving in and out of the apple trees now, trying to keep hidden.

I was going in the wrong direction, deeper into the orchard and isolated farmland. I wanted to move towards the house, but he cut off that route. I had to either get to the canal so that I could run unnoticed back to the house or run through the orchard and face the deadly prospect of Dickenson hiding in the trees, waiting. The prospect of being his target wasn't appealing at all. Another hundred yards down the bank. No opening. The brush was too thick to get to the canal path. I was running out of time. I decided to make a run for it through the orchard.

I looked for Dickenson and didn't see him. That made me nervous. I crouched on the bank. If I could get to the other side of the orchard in one piece, I was reasonably safe. I could zig zag through the trees. There were a couple of barns over there. If I could get across the road, I could run into Newport. Newport was only a mile away. Forget the truck. Forget the phone. Get to town and get Munger. Maybe find a house along the way and use their phone. Good plan. All I had to do is move.

"Maxwell, I know you are out there. Come on out, now." Holy shit, he was closer than I thought. I hunched lower into the ditch. I finally saw him come out from under an apple tree. He was about fifty feet away. I picked up a small rock and threw it as hard as I could down the ditch. He fired three shots at the spot where it hit a tree. I used the distraction to jump out of the ditch and head towards the orchard. There was about twenty feet of open space between me and the first tree. His next shot stopped me in my tracks. I heard a puff of air as it passed my head. The side of my head exploded. The impact knocked me to the ground. I could feel wetness pouring down my face. I felt the blood and realized that I was still alive. The shot grazed me and dazed me for a few seconds. I jumped up and ran towards a large old apple tree. I heard a couple more shots and hoped my luck would hold out. Under the tree, I used my shirt to wipe the blood and sweat off my face. I was having trouble seeing, and I was feeling light-headed.

I tried to hide behind the trunk of the tree. It didn't provide much cover, and Dickenson was getting closer. I wiped more blood and tried to think. The other edge of the orchard seemed to be a hundred miles away and getting further every minute. But if I stood here any longer, I was for sure dead. I couldn't think. I decided to climb the tree. If I could get in the right position, if my luck held out, maybe I could jump him. I grabbed the first branch and hoisted myself up. I was trying to shinny up the back of the tree so that he could not see me. I was about six feet off the ground when he burst under the tree. He ran around back expecting to find me on the ground. I grabbed the next branch to pull myself higher. He heard me and looked up. He fired his gun just as I was putting all my weight on the upper branch. I felt the bullet hit me in the chest. The impact slammed me into the trunk of the tree, pulling the branch with me. I heard it give. A loud crack, and I was tumbling out of the tree. I pulled the branch with me. The branch ripped from the tree, pulling me in a circle, and as I fell, I threw it like a spear. I hit the ground face first. I was going to die under this tree. That bastard Dickenson was going to get away. He was going to kill Aunt Liz, he was going to kill Kim, and he was going to take my boat. A sudden surge of anger gave me the strength to turn over. I was lying on my back. I couldn't get up. I looked for Dickenson. I waited for him to finish me off. Blood ran into my eyes, and I could not see. The pain in my chest overcame me, and as the world began to darken around me, I could hear the wind rustling the apple leaves. I closed my eyes, waiting for the end.

THIRTY-TWO

When I opened my eyes again, it was night. I could see the stars twinkling through the apple branches. There was a cloud moving slowly across the moonlit sky. A soft breeze chilled me. I shivered, and the pain returned. The pain was both overwhelming and comforting. I was alive. Without notice, it began to subside as I watched as clouds and stars began to spin. Faster and faster. Gray and black turned to yellow and blue, and green and red. Spinning into a white light. A bright light that blinded me. I blinked a couple times. When I could see again, the apple orchard was gone, the night was gone, and the pain was gone. The sun was shining, and I was standing in a stand of ancient pine trees, on the outer edge of a large meadow. The meadow was surrounded by prehistoric pine trees. The smell was of primordial earth, and Christmas. In the middle of the tall grass, and Queen Anne's lace, stood a man and a woman. The sun appeared to be shining directly on them as bees buzzed and butterflies fluttered around them. They were facing each other holding both hands. Two lovers together again. I could feel their love and relief that they were finally together again. I felt their joy. I tried to focus. I wanted to see who it was. I wanted to know where I was. As I was trying to clear my vision, another couple walked out from a well-worn path in the pines on the far side of the meadow. They looked familiar, but I couldn't see their faces. They were holding hands. I moved my hand to clear my eyes. The pain sent the darkness back and the meadow began to spin and move farther away. The bright light dimmed. The blue and yellow twirled. Pain returned. I wiped wetness from my eyes and put my hand down. The meadow stopped spinning. I could see more clearly. In the tall grass stood Aunt Liz and Uncle Bud. They were now embracing, so happy to see each other. They were talking but I couldn't hear what they were saying. I watched as the other couple came closer. They embraced Aunt Liz also, and then turned to me. Jim and Diane Maxwell. They turned and looked at me. I felt like I was ten again. My mother waved at me, I called out her name. She smiled. I could see her lips move. I couldn't hear her. I called again, louder. Pain returned. The shadows threatened. The two couples walked towards the path on the other side of the meadow. I screamed. The meadow began to spin again. The white light blinded, eventually fading into blue and yellow and green. I opened my eyes again and could only see the apple tree leaves shaking the stars and the moonlit sky. I could only feel the pain. I tried to move, I wanted to get up, to follow them down that path. Once again, I lost consciousness.

THIRTY-THREE

The mid-morning sun, rising over the apple trees and peeking through the branches, burned through my closed eyelids. I tried to move. Pain reported in from every inch of my body. If I stayed perfectly still, I could almost breathe pain-free. I looked around. I moved my head, the darkness threatened again. I fought it. I could see somebody lying about twenty feet away. I tried to move. I couldn't make anything happen. As my memory of yesterday's events returned, I got scared. I had been shot by a madman who was now probably on his way to Canada on my boat. I couldn't move. There was nothing I could do about it. It came to me that I was probably going to die out here in this orchard. I wanted to save Aunt Liz and failed. Now, probably, Kim was in danger too. He was going to get her next, he said. As for me, I was in trouble. Nobody knew I was out here. It hurt to breathe. I could taste blood. The gunshot in my chest probably messed up something bad. I closed my eyes. More spinning, more bright light. I was standing on the edge of the meadow again. I looked across to the path into the pines on the other side. There was nobody around. I called for my parents. I called for Aunt Liz and Uncle Bud. Nothing. I screamed. From the path, I heard a voice. "Over here. He's over here." I tried to cross the meadow. I couldn't move. It hurt to move. I was delirious. I could see the meadow on the other side of the trees; the bees were flying around the dandelions and clover. Suddenly two of them turned towards me and started flying my way. I closed my eyes. The path disappeared, and the orchard came out. When I reopened them, giant bees were hovering around me. They kept yelling, "He's over here!" I tried to smile when one stuck its face in my face. I just snarled. "He's still alive," one yelled.

"Armset totem mike?" I wanted to know who he was talking about. "Argent freeson polt." I continued. I wanted to tell the bees about Dickenson. Maybe I could still save Kim. They didn't respond. It seemed perfectly normal to be talking to a giant bee. He grabbed me, and I passed out. I kept fading in and out of consciousness, and this created a collage of different images that all blended together. When I opened my eyes again, the bees were gone, and Jack Munger was walking next to me. We were moving, but I was still lying down. I remembered Dickenson saying that he was probably at the Towner in front of a plate of donuts. He was talking. I tried to understand what he said. He had a small jelly stain on the expanse of official uniform that covered his belly. I tried to laugh, finding it hilarious, that Munger was eating jelly donuts while we were all dying in the orchard. The effort made me choke and pass out. It also made the head bee begin yelling and the stretcher-bearers move faster. Several police officers were carrying me somewhere. They melted into the roof of the ambulance, and the screaming of a siren, which blended into a large white light that blinded me. I started to look again for the meadow. All I saw were green masked bugs hovering around. The head bug said, "Let's get him under. We don't have much time." I wanted to ask him what he meant. I decided that the green bugs were going to bury me. I wasn't dead yet. I started to protest. I tried to move. When I tried to tell the head bug that I was still alive, another bug covered my face. It felt like a muzzle. I started to feel sleepy, and good. The pain was subsiding. I decided that if this was how it felt being buried, I would let them do it. Let the bugs win. I felt myself slip away.

When I opened my eyes again. I was lying on a bed, in a white room. A hospital room. There was a beeping sound in my right ear and a strange woman in green scrubs standing next to me. She was making some adjustments to the thing that was beeping.

"Welcome back, we were beginning to wonder if you were ever going to come back." She said as she noticed me moving. I tried to talk, but there was something in my mouth. "Don't try to talk. You are hooked up to more hoses and wires than the space shuttle." I tried to understand what she was talking about. I couldn't move very much, but I tried to look around. I was in a hospital room. I was alive. The green bugs didn't bury me. The door to the room opened. In walked Kim. I tried to snarl. All I ended up doing was coughing around the breathing tube. I was so excited to see her. She was carrying a cup of coffee, which she dropped when she saw that I was awake. There was a lot of commotion and I couldn't see what was going on, but

Kim and the doctor were cleaning up the coffee. With a metal chart in one hand, and a trashcan filled with paper towels in the other, the green scrubbed doctor left the room, leaving us alone. Kim tried to hug me. She couldn't find a good way to do it, so she just kissed me on the forehead. I never felt anything so nice. She then tried to bring me up to date.

"Jack Munger called me when they put you into the ambulance. I met them all here. We are in the intensive care department of Strong Hospital. They said when you woke up, they would take the tube out. I will get them to do that so we can talk. You were brought here by ambulance. They operated right away. You were in surgery all day. All I did was pray. I have been here ever since. Evie said to take as long as I needed. You have been in a coma for about a week." I was out for a week. It seemed like only a couple of hours. I started to cry. She continued. "They fixed the damage that the bullet did to your chest. Fortunately, it missed any important arteries, or organs." I wondered which ones were not important. "They also patched up your head. There was a large gouge out of it. You lost a lot of blood. You could have died out there." I nodded. "The thing is that there is an infection that they cannot seem to get under control."

I wanted to ask a million questions. About Aunt Liz. About Earle. About Dickenson, and my boat. I was glad at least that he hadn't followed through with this plan to kill Kim. I tried with my eyes to ask everything. Kim didn't understand. Finally, she said, "I know you have a million questions, but they will have to wait until the tube comes out." I looked sad and started to cry. "Don't worry baby, I ain't goin' nowhere, and neither are you. We will have plenty of time to talk." I tried to give her the snarl-smile again. She was holding my hand as I fell back to sleep. I hoped she would be there when I woke up.

THIRTY-FOUR

They woke me, not an hour later, to take out the tube. It hurt. But I was glad to have it out. I looked for Kim. She was sitting in the corner. Away from the activity. My voice sounded raspy as I said hi. I tried to wave. She just smiled and waved. The room was filled with doctors and nurses, all busy. They were checking bandages and asking questions. One doctor kept asking my name. I kept repeating it. I asked for a glass of water. He got concerned when I couldn't tell him what day it was. He kept asking. Kim spoke up when she saw my frustration level rise. She reminded him that I had been in a coma all week. How in the hell was I going to know what day it was? I could hear anger in her voice. The doctor backed down. He started asking other questions. Birthday, where did I live, etc. I must have answered these questions right, because everyone was smiling. Everyone except one doctor standing on the outer edge of the commotion, looking at a chart. Apparently satisfied, everyone left the room except for this one doctor. And Kim.

"Mr. Maxwell. I want to talk to you about your condition," she turned to Kim. "Can you excuse us please?" She looked towards the door.

"I'm not going anywhere," Kim replied. She stood and assumed a fighting stance. I could see the fire in her eyes again. "Whatever you tell him, you can tell me."

"Ma'am, by law I can only discuss Mr. Maxwell's condition with him, or his spouse. Or family members."

"And me."

"It's ok," I rasped.

"Mr. Maxwell..."

"It is ok," Kim interrupted. "Mr. Maxwell has no family or spouse. I have been designated by the hospital to be his advocate." I didn't know that. I just wanted her there. My head was kind of fuzzy. Somebody needed to ask the right questions. She pulled a card out of her pocket and handed it to the doctor. "If you have any problems, call this guy." I didn't see the card, but it seemed to satisfy the doctor. She nodded. Kim stepped up and grabbed my hand. "I told you I wasn't going anywhere."

"Very well," the doctor said. She glanced once more at my chart and snapped it shut. I could actually see her take on her professional persona. She was wearing a pair of half-glasses. She took them off and pointed them at me. "Now, Mr. Maxwell, you are a lucky man."

"Not feeling too lucky."

"You should. You were shot twice. Once in the head, and once in the chest. There was a lot of blood loss. The bullet that hit your head just grazed your skull leaving a groove that will be permanent. Fortunately, it will be under the hairline. The amazing thing is that it didn't fracture the bone.'

"Hard-headed, I guess." I tried to laugh. All I ended up doing was coughing. Kim just smiled. The doctor didn't react at all, waiting impatiently for me to finish so she could continue. I took a drink of water.

"The bullet that hit your chest, hit right above your right lung. Amazingly, again, between the lung and the bones of your shoulder. There is a lot of muscle and tissue damage, but nothing serious. The fascinating thing is that if either bullet was even an inch from where it was, you would be dead. A game of inches. I keep saying that the ER game is a game of inches. One inch between life, and death," she stopped talking. She seemed embarrassed by the show of emotion. I was impressed by the passion that she displayed. I gained a new respect.

"Doctor?"

"Yes?"

"What is your name?"

"Dr. Lora." Kim couldn't resist an outburst of laughter. "Yeah, like the radio lady. Not spelled the same." She softened a little. She smiled at Kim. "My husband's family has a name about twenty letters long. When they came through Ellis Island, it was shortened to Lora."

Kim asked, "Dr. Lora, where do we go from here?" She had moved back to the side of the bed and was holding my hand again.

"Like I said, you are a lucky man, Mr. Maxwell. The bullet wounds should heal without any major problems. With physical therapy, your shoulder should recover full mobility. What I am concerned about is the infection. We are going to pump you full of drugs and keep a close eye on you until we can get that under control." With that, her beeper went off. Once again, she took on that harried look that hospital doctors all seem to wear. After promising to check in often, she ran out of the room.

The infection was a problem. Later that night, my fever spiked, and the delirium returned. I was waffling between the hospital and the meadow, and nurses and Dr. Lora took turns being large bugs. In the meadow, I kept looking for Aunt Liz and Uncle Bud. I called for my parents. I must have been yelling out loud. That sent the entire medical staff scurrying. Between the fever and the pain medication, the next two weeks were a blur. Day and night blended with the opening and closing of my eyes. Kim was always there but kept turning into Dr. Lora, into a nurse, back to Kim, into Jack Munger, into a couple of men in black suits, back into Kim. They were all talking to me, and I remember responding, but I don't remember what was said. Kim kept turning into other people. Munger again, a young woman in a business suit, and a heavyset guy with a cheesy mustache dressed in jeans and a flannel shirt. We all spent a lot of time talking. I remembered a conversation with Johnny Good. They all had something to say. I remembered bits and pieces. Earle was dead. So was Aunt Liz. Dickenson too. I think they told me all about it, but I just can't remember. It all made me sad.

It was a Friday morning, I found out later. The sun was shining through the hospital window onto the bed. It woke me up. For the first time in days, my mind was clear. I could think. I could feel pain. I looked around the room. It was a white room with green curtains. Nobody was there but me. The constant rhythm of the IV pump was the only sound. I tried to recall what was going on, but my last full memory was of the conversation with Dr. Lora and Kim. I couldn't tell even how long ago that was. Everything else was a blur.

I wondered what day it was. What time it was. Where was Kim? I was wide-awake. The fever had broken sometime in the night, the meds finally kicking the invading infection from my body. With less and less pain, I was on less pain medicine also. I moved my right arm. Stiffness but no pain. I checked the wounded areas. There was a small bandage on my head. And a slightly larger one on my chest. My head didn't hurt when I touched it; my chest did. I tried moving other parts of my body. I felt frail. Like I was 80 years old, not 35.

I spent the rest of the morning with the nursing staff in and out. I found out that it had been two weeks since the conversation with Dr. Lora. That it was indeed Friday morning. Early Friday morning. That I hadn't eaten in two weeks, hence the IV. That they were glad to see that the fever broke. I asked about Kim. They said that she wasn't in yet. I guess that I assumed she was staying here all the time, but maybe it just seemed like it in my confused, infected mind. I told them I was hungry, and they all got excited. A tray was suddenly in front of me, and I instantly regretted my comments as I looked at the cold eggs and soggy bacon. I decided to wait.

Some of it started to come back to me as I lay in bed. Aunt Liz was dead. This fact began to sink in, and I started to cry. I couldn't save her after all. In fact, it was she that saved me. Without her diversion, we would both be dead now. Maybe Kim too. I tried to hold it in but the tears started to flow. I was glad that I was alone. All my life, Aunt Liz was there. She was my safety net. She was so good at it that I didn't realize she was doing that. The good ones, the good parents create that safety net. Not so that the child is protected from everything, but so that the child's exposure to a world that is more than willing to roll right over them is real. So good that I believed I didn't need her help. So good at it that I was able to shun her for five years, and she forgave me. I started sobbing. I turned my back on her and look where that got me. Broke and divorced, unable to work. As I lay there, I realized that every time I got into trouble over the years, she was there. When I fell off my bike in the road when I was twelve, she came running. When Missy Caleb broke my heart in high school, she sat with me. Cried with me. Then told me to go find a better girl. Even recently when we were pulled over by Dickenson on our way to the Clinton's. She stuck up for 'her kid.' Finally, one of her final acts on this earth: it was her scream that created the diversion that I needed to get loose. That act freed me. But I couldn't get back to her. I cried as I remembered. Then I remembered the words she used after the Missy Caleb incident. Words that described Aunt Liz to a 't'. "All right," she had said. "You have had your cry, now get on with it." This was a little heavier than a teenaged broken heart, but I decided that the best way that I could honor her life was to 'get on with it.' I remembered then that someone had said that Aunt Liz had been cremated, like Uncle Bud, and that the service would be held when I was healthy enough to have it. The tears were dried up, and I was trying to get a nurse to bring me a hot lunch when Kim walked in with Jack Munger.

"Look who I found," she said. She kissed me on the forehead. "I talked to Dr. Lora. She said you are doing better today."

"Yeah, when I woke up today, it was like the light

finally came on. They say that my temp is headed towards normal, and I am hungry. That seems to make everybody very happy. How are you, Jack?"

"Maxwell, they tell me you are one lucky sombitch." He pulled a chair from the other side of the room and sat down. He let out a deep sigh, as if the air was being let out of a marshmallow.

"Yeah, that's what they tell me too."

"I just want to clear up what we talked about the other day. And put this investigation to bed."

"I gotta be honest, Jack; I don't really remember much of what we talked about the other day. Dickenson is dead, I know that. I don't know how."

"Really? You don't know? You don't remember?" He moved to the edge of his seat. He was surprised. "You got him."

It was my turn to be shocked. "Me?"

"That's the best we can figure. You are the only one to survive that mess, and you can't remember. We found him about twenty feet away from you. There was a tree branch sticking out of his left eye. He was dead. The way we got it figured was that you were up in a tree. When we saw the branch, we tried to figure out where it came from. We found the tree, your blood was on it, the bullet was still in the trunk and the branch fit perfectly a spot where one had been broken off. The best guess we can make is that you somehow broke the branch off and threw it at him. Like I said, lucky sombitch."

"I was up in that tree. My plan was to get around him and run into town. He saw me right away and shot me. I grabbed a branch to keep from falling and it broke. Next thing I remember for sure was being carried out on the stretcher." I decided not to tell anyone about the meadow. "I guess climbing that tree was a bad idea."

"I don't know. That god dam branch took a one-in-a-million flight path."

"You got the bad guy," said Kim.

"Yeah." I got the bad guy. I killed a man. I didn't know what to think about that. On the one hand, I 'got the bad guy.' Dickenson was dead and was not going to hurt anyone else. On the other hand, he was dead because I killed him. I just couldn't shake the Judeo-Christian moral stand that all life was sacred. That was how I was brought up. I tried to smile. I tried to feel good about it, but deep in my stomach, down in the pits where real feelings lie, I couldn't help but feel like I did something bad. Really bad. Like going to hell bad. I needed to talk to Johnny. He might be able to put the whole thing in perspective. I had a question. "Munger, why did it take you so long to get to Earle's place?"

"We were running all around town that day. We had a sheriff down at the marina looking for you. We had a car in front of the library, and at Kim's house. We were looking for Earle also. We thought he might have finally skipped town. I sent Dickenson out to his house to find him. He kept calling in, regular as clockwork that there was no sign of Earle, or you, or anything. We didn't come out there because we thought we had that base covered." He shifted in his chair. He hung his head. "Obviously that wasn't so."

"How would you know," said Kim. "How would you know that it was your own guy? Dickenson was a creep, but he wasn't a crook, or a killer. At least as far as anyone knew. You were right to trust him." Munger looked like a kid just saved from the switch. He even smiled.

I thought about the money. "Did you find any money?"

"We found about a hundred grand, give or take," he said. "There was a bag in the barn, all cash. We are trying to get an accounting of everyone's contribution. So that when this investigation is done, we can return it. I would think that after I write up a report of our conversation today, that would close the case. I guess that some would come to you, now. No one knows how much there was, but we believe that this was the most of it, with the rest being spent." I thought differently but didn't say anything.

THIRTY-FIVE

It was a week later, May 21st, when I was finally discharged from the hospital. When the fever broke, recovery was pretty fast. I became restless. I wanted to go home. After I proved that I could walk farther than the nurse's station and not get worn out. After I threw a plate of Jell-O at an orderly, they decided that it was time to go. I couldn't wait, and was up and dressed by 8 AM, waiting for Kim to come get me. She didn't show up until ten. By the time we signed all the papers, said goodbye to Doctor Lora, and got the mandatory wheelchair ride to the door, it was noon.

The walk to Kim's Prius was longer than the trips around the nurses' station, and I was tired when I got to her parking spot. Kim was chatty as we pulled out of the hospital parking garage, talking about little things. She talked about the drive from Newport, the weather; she talked about Evie, and the library, and her extended leave of absence. She talked about helping me convalesce. She wanted to stop on the way home for lunch. I was only half listening as I watched the world go by. It had only been a few weeks, but it seemed like I was in that hospital room forever. Before that, I was lost in a dream world. As we drove through the city, I thought about the meadow, and watching Aunt Liz, Uncle Bud and my parents meet up. Was that a dream? It felt so real. Kim chattered on as I tried to remember details, like: was it cold or hot? Was there a breeze? Was there any sound? I let my mind wander as we cruised out 390 towards the Lake Ontario State Parkway. Kim's voice brought me back to the here and now. She said, "...I hope you like what we did."

"Like what?" She brought me back to the real world.

"Dale and I cleaned up Bella and stocked her for a long voyage, just like you said."

"Kim," I looked at her as if she was crazy. "What are we talking about?"

"Your boat. Don't you remember?" I was in a completely new area here. I didn't remember anything about my boat. All I knew was that I couldn't wait to get home to the marina, and I was looking forward to getting aboard and taking a nap.

"No, I don't. What happened to my boat?"

"Oh boy." She pulled off the expressway. We were almost to the parkway, but we pulled onto the off ramp. There was a small diner near the exit, and she pulled up front. "This is one of my favorite places. Let's get some lunch." She got out of the car and walked in. She turned to me, I hadn't moved yet. "C'mon. I'm hungry." I got out of the car. All of a sudden, I was in a bad mood. I was tired, and all I wanted to do was get home. To my bunk, and sleep. Now Kim was talking about a conversation about my boat. I didn't remember. My mood soured by the idea that

I might have made some decisions while under the influence of the high fever. I got worried that there might be other things I didn't remember. Reluctantly, I got out of the car. Kim was already seated at a booth, ordering two cups of coffee. I sat down and looked at her. "You really don't remember?"

"Kim, I really don't remember."

"You decided that the best way to recover was to sail Bella around the lake. You told me about the cash under your bed and had me get her ready." She looked incredulous. "You really don't remember?" I shook my head. "You even told me to get Dale Jr. to help. He was very helpful. You said you wanted me to go with you." She looked unsure.

As she was telling me this, I remembered a little about the conversation. I couldn't remember when it was. It seemed like a great idea. Kim and I, around the lake for the rest of the summer. We could explore every bay and port. We could sail up into the thousand islands. I really couldn't think of a better way to regain my strength. My mood lightened. Then I wondered, "What else don't I remember?" I asked her to tell me everything that happened.

"Well, the first week you had a lot of visitors." The waitress approached the table. We both ordered cheeseburgers; mine was a double. It all smelled so good, and after the food that hospital served, I wanted some real food. I got fries, and a salad, and a milkshake. Kim looked at me with surprise. "Let's recap," she stated as the waitress went away. "Do you remember Miss Carson?" I shook my head. "Ok. She is a lawyer."

"Was she the young woman in the black business

suit?"

"You do remember."

"Why was she there?"

"She came as a representative of the law firm that held your Aunt's will. With the exception of a small percentage left to the church, you are the sole heir. She felt that you should know, I guess. You can meet with her as soon as you are ready."

I did remember bits and pieces of this conversation. She was a pretty, young girl, and I didn't think she looked old enough to be a real lawyer. She talked about a lot of things that I already knew. From our conversation on the porch, I knew the basics of Aunt Liz's estate, and was in no hurry to deal with it. I figured it might be better to bury her first. Then worry about her assets. "What about Aunt Liz?"

"Her will stipulated that she be cremated, like your uncle. And buried next to him, of course. The funeral home in Newport took care of that and is holding her remains, awaiting your instructions."

"I remember a couple of guys in suits. Like the Men in Black, or something. Does that sound right?

"Yeah, they were there with Jack. One was a state police investigator and the other was with the sheriff's office." She was working steadily on the burger that was in front of her. My plate sat untouched. I was not as hungry as I thought. "You must remember that. They made you go over it and over it again and again until you told them all in no uncertain terms to go have sex with themselves. I had to laugh at that, and even Jack was smiling, but those two were not amused."

I was having a real problem with the idea that I was

thinking and talking and apparently cursing out cops and had no memory of it. The good thing was that with this conversation, it was coming back. Those two guys were first class jerks, but they were thorough. They kept asking the same questions over and over again, and as soon I realized their tactic was to try to trip me up, it became a game. Not only did I tell them the same thing over and over again, I used the same words. It was easy. I was telling the truth. That pissed them off. Everybody is guilty in a cop's eyes and should be running scared. I didn't scare. I had nothing to hide. I didn't kill anybody, at least intentionally, and was the only living victim. They tried to trip me up and couldn't. They went away mad, but apparently went away satisfied. Jack said the investigation was done and they were closing the case. As we sat in the booth, I looked out the window and got angry again, that I had to go through that inquisition. I decided to talk to Jack about it, and maybe the cute lawyer. I took a few bites of my burger. The fries had gone cold, and I pushed them aside. I wasn't as hungry as a thought. I remembered one more person in the room. "Kim, there was another guy. Flannel? Does that sound right?"

She took a couple of minutes. "Yes," she practically jumped out of her seat. "I forgot about him."

"Who was he?"

"He came with Reverend Good." Johnny had been there a couple of times. I remembered his visits. One visit was when Kim was not around, and we talked for a couple of hours, about God, life, Kim, and Aunt Liz. "Do you remember when you were at the Goods the day before you were shot?"

"Yeah."

"Do you remember him talking about a guy from Ohio?"

"You mean the minster?"

"No, apparently there was a guy from Earle's church out there. I can't remember his name. You will have to ask Reverend Good. Anyway, he came out to claim Earle's body and escort it back to Ohio. I thought that was kinda weird." I couldn't remember his name either. "He just showed up one morning. Wanted to make sure you were ok."

I wasn't ok. Nowhere near it. I had been shot. I almost died. I felt fifty pounds lighter and walked like an old man. I tired easily, and it hurt to move my shoulder. I just wanted to go home. I needed to rest. I needed to start the long process of recovery. I had witnessed death. He had actually tried to kill me, but I was the one that came out alive. But I didn't feel invincible. Lucky, maybe. In fact, today, I didn't even feel lucky. I felt like the smallest sound wave, the smallest breeze, would cause all of the tiny little threads that held me together to snap, and all the parts that used to be me would be lying in a pile on the floor of this diner. All this day's activity was sapping my energy, fast. Kim sensed what I was thinking, and after paying the check, helped me to the car. I must have fallen asleep as she drove, as my next memory was of the Newport off ramp.

We arrived at the marina. Dale Jr. saw us pull in and came out of the store to greet us. He wanted to tell me all about the things they did to ready Bella for our cruise, but Kim cut him short. He could tell me another time. He looked disappointed. At that point I didn't care. I could already feel my bed. I could smell the river. I could hear the lake washing up on the shore, hear the tick –tick –tick, of rigging against aluminum masts. I was happy. I started down the steps toward the docks. Kim apologized again to Dale Jr. and raced to catch up with me.

Bella looked different as I approached. Like she had missed me and was glad to see me. Like she had put on her Sunday best to welcome me home. She was as clean as I had ever seen her, and there was the feeling of celebration as I entered. She was well-stocked. There were stores everywhere. I looked in the cupboards and fridge. They were full. I wanted to leave right then. Kim suggested that we might want to wait until I could get through the day without a nap first. She was right, plus there was some business to be taken care of. When I yawned instead of arguing, she just nodded knowingly and pointed towards my cabin. Passively I went in, stripped down, and crawled into bed. Kim crawled in with me and put her arms around me. I was home.

THIRTY-SIX

I was alone when I woke up. The boat was silent. The kind of silence that screams emptiness. I listened to hear Kim bustling in the galley, but there was nothing. I got up, and like an old man, tottered my way out to the galley. She was gone. I fixed a strong gin and tonic and took a sip. I couldn't remember anything that tasted so good. I took another. I opened the right top drawer under the counter. This is where I kept my supply of Garcia Vegas. There was a fresh box. Kim had thought of everything. As I unwrapped one, I thought about how Cindy used to tell me that these were going to kill me. After the last month, I hoped I lived long enough that I had to worry about that. I lit one. I took another sip of gin. I was wrong. This tasted even better. I realized that I was hungry. I ate the rest of the cheeseburger from lunch. I threw out the cold fries.

I wondered where Kim was. I walked out into the cockpit and looked around. She was sitting on the bench where she was waiting for me that first night we had dinner. That seemed like a lifetime ago. It was only about four weeks. She looked as beautiful, and I couldn't help but wonder how I got so lucky. How we got so deep. She was going to take the summer off to be with me. The crazy thing was that, although I knew I should not let her take that much time off from the library, I couldn't imagine how I would get through it without her. She was talking to Dale Jr. I walked over to them. At the same time, they noticed me, and turned to face me. They stopped talking as I approached.

"It's good to see you up and about, Mr. Maxwell," said Dale. He stood and shook my hand.

"You slept well?" Kim rose and kissed me. I wasn't sure, but I thought I saw Dale look disappointed. He looked away. I just smiled and kissed her back.

"I feel better," I said. "Dale, I wanted to thank you for all you did on Bella." I pointed with the cigar towards the marina parking lot. "I am sorry about Ol' Betsy too. I know I dented her up. Was it bad?"

"You're welcome Mr. Maxwell; it was fun getting your boat ready." He smiled at Kim. She didn't notice. "As for my truck, I am revoking your rental agreement." He laughed. "You did a pretty good job on her. The box is wrecked, and I think that the frame is bent. She is in the barn across the street, and I have the box off. A friend of mine thinks he can straighten out the frame, at least make her useable for plowing and boat hauling. I think her rental days are done, though."

"You just tell me what it will cost, and I will cover it."

"I don't know what that number will be. I am trying to find a new box now, but they are few and far between."

"I'll tell you what, I'll get you some cash and we'll see

how far that goes, ok?" He nodded. "So, tell me what you guys did to pretty up my Bella." They looked at each other, and their faces lit up like kids with Christmas presents. They both started talking at the same time. We all laughed.

"You tell him, Dale," Kim said.

"What I did was approach it like it was my own boat. If I was going to go on an extended trip, I would want to make sure everything was ship-shape. So, I took her out and tested everything, making a list of what needed to be fixed. There were a couple of lines that looked suspicious, your GPS and auto-pilot weren't working. After that, there were just a couple of little things that just needed a little TLC. She is in pretty good shape, but she was showing the wear and tear that one might expect from your trip up from Florida. Man, I still want to do that someday." He looked wistful. I didn't know that the autopilot wasn't working. I hadn't used it since I left Florida. "When I brought her back in, I hauled her and had a couple guys paint the bottom. When we put her back in, Kim cleaned up the inside and stocked her. I did all the maintenance. She is ready now, for anything, I guarantee." He was smiling and self-satisfied, as he finished his narrative. I decided that I liked this kid.

"And it's all paid for," added Kim. I thanked them both and wondered just how much of my stash was left. I decided not to ruin the moment with those kinds of questions. The phone in the marina store started ringing. It sounded like the bell at the old grammar school, announcing that class was over. Dale excused himself and went to tend to his business.

Kim and I went back to Bella. It was warm enough to sit in the cockpit. The sun was starting to set and the sky to the west was bright salmon. Clouds passed overhead to the east, as if they were chasing the daylight. There were more boats in the marina than when I was last there. I suspected that a lot of Dale Jr.'s work this time of year had to do with putting boats in the water. Some boats were bigger than Bella, some smaller, but they all looked clean and ready to go. We sat alone, though, as none were occupied. Most were still covered with winter tarps. I was glad we were alone. I wasn't ready for people yet. Kim was enough.

Kim fixed us both a drink and resettled into the cockpit. She sat with her legs tucked under. Facing me. We talked quietly. We talked about our trip. We decided that we needed to take care of some business before we left. There was the matter of Aunt Liz's funeral. We had to do something with her house. I guess it was my house now. I wondered what to do with it. I couldn't imagine living there. There was a meeting with Miss Carson. There was also the question of my health. Kim would not leave until she was sure that I was able to handle the boat by myself. Over and over she kept saying that she didn't know anything about boats and argued that she wasn't going to be out on the lake with somebody that was going to drop dead at any minute. I argued that I was already strong enough, and we reached a compromise. When I could walk to the lake and back from the marina, we would leave. I thought that would be a good measure. I would have to teach Kim the fundamentals. There is a certain amount of work in sailing a boat around the lake, and I couldn't do it all. But it was all no big deal, I was feeling pretty good at the moment. Well rested. I figured that I would be able to start all that tomorrow.

We sat for a while talking as a couple does. We talked about just about everything. We talked about nothing. We were silent, just happy in each other's company. Finally, Kim decided that two drinks were enough and that we should begin thinking about turning in. I was yawning my agreement when I saw a tall man walking down the dock. It was getting dark, and I couldn't tell who it was until he got closer.

"Aren't you out past your bedtime, Reverend?"

"Arnie, is that you?" He stood at attention and made a mock salute. "Permission to come aboard, Captain?"

`I think I said something about some people not having any class. He responded. "I don't understand how you could bring such a pretty girl onto an old tub like this. Don't you got any respect?" He turned to Kim, "If I was you, I would run. Run. Now while you still can." They both were laughing. I was trying to figure out why they were so chummy. It was like he could read my mind. "We met at the hospital. Don't you remember? We spent almost a whole afternoon together." I had to admit that I didn't remember that afternoon. Kim was nodding agreement. I accepted.

"So, what does bring a man of the cloth from far off lands way out here this late in the day?"

"I was in Newport. I am going to resign my church in Lockport and move back home. I always wanted to come back to that church. They approached me shortly after Earle died to help out. One thing led to another, and I was in Newport getting approved for the job."

"Well, this calls for a celebration." I stood up. And sat right back down again. I didn't have any strength left.

"Maybe we can celebrate later." Kim looked at Johnny

and shared that mother hen look. We sat in the cockpit quietly talking for a little while longer, I couldn't stop yawning.

"It's getting late," Johnny said. "I better be going." Kim gave him a hug, and I managed to get to my feet to hug him also. "Glad you are home. Glad you are alive, my friend." He stepped off the boat and waved as he walked away.

When he was no longer in sight, Kim and I went below. I headed back towards the captain's quarters. It took me five minutes to shed my clothes and crawl back under the covers. I had no energy. I didn't want to talk. I couldn't even think. I put my hands on my chest and stared at the ceiling. I could hear Kim in the other room, putting things away, getting ready for bed. Finally, she came into the room. She was wearing one of my old t-shirts. "Yes, I can" was written across her chest. Her hair was pulled back into a ponytail. I snarled at the sight. I tried to come up with a clever quip. I got nothing. My heart started pumping faster, and I couldn't wait to feel the girl-weight on the other side of the bed. She dug her way under the blankets and snuggled into my chest. As my eyes were closing, she rolled on top of me. "I am glad you are alive too, my friend." With that, she kissed me, and rolled back off. She snuggled again into my chest. As I started to fall asleep, I looked around. Kim's stuff was everywhere. I closed my eyes, knowing that when I woke up tomorrow, she would still be there. I put my arm around her and let myself drift off.

THIRTY-SEVEN

Despite the strong, northeasterly wind, the August air felt still. After breakfast, we pushed out of the Genesee River, past Charlotte Beach heading west. Heading home. I set the autopilot to a course that had us more or less pointing at Toronto. My plan was to make one long tack sailing this course until we could see the Canadian coast, then a straight run into Saunders Point. After a long summer of crisscrossing the lake, we were heading home. We were in no hurry, and I had the sails set wide open. I wished I had a spinnaker. Kim was down below cleaning up breakfast. Tomorrow was Labor Day, and we decided to make this, the last leg of our summer on the lake, last all day. I was sitting in the cockpit by the wheel. One eye was on the autopilot, the other was on the screen of my laptop, opened to Word. I had been writing the entire trip. Every day, a little more. A story that I might not believe if it was written by Patterson or Grisham.

It was a full two weeks after I got out of the hospital

that we were able to finally set sail. On a morning not unlike today, we passed the end of the rocky piers, and with a silent nod to my happy place, set a course due north. Those days before we left were filled with activity. Each day began with a walk to the lake. It was almost a week before I could make it to the lake and back and not collapse from exhaustion from the effort. I knew that I was going to be ok, when on the fifth day, instead of heading back to my cabin for a nap alone, I took Kim by the hand and took her with me. For the first time since I was shot, we made love. The tension had been building, and a couple of times we started, only to stop when I completely ran out of steam. The mind was willing, as the saying goes. When we finally reached that moment with all its anticipation, it exceeded all expectations. Kim was gentle and caring, making sure not to overdo. She took control both giving pleasure, and receiving pleasure, in what had to be the most sensual experience of my life. As we lay, afterwards, glistening from exertion, me barely awake and exhausted, we looked into each other's eyes. I wanted to tell her that I loved her but said nothing; she just smiled and said she already knew. She also declared that we were adding one more exercise to my daily routine. I suggested maybe twice a day.

Aunt Liz was buried on a Tuesday. Johnny Good performed the funeral, and once again, I marveled at the passion and emotion with which he worked. The Newport Presbyterian church was filled with her friends. We travelled out to the Newport cemetery, and after Johnny read from Genesis, I lowered the small plastic box into the ground. After a reception back at the church, Kim and I went with the Goods and met a bunch of people from the lakefront at the Old North Inn. We all took turns buying shots and drinking to her memory. I guess I had a few more than I should, and I didn't notice when Johnny left. We were the last to leave. I passed out in the car. When we got back to the marina, Kim left me sleeping in the car.

The rest of our days were spent taking care of business. We met with Miss Carson regarding Aunt Liz's estate. There was the house and the car and bank accounts, which were almost emptied out by Reverend Earle and Dickenson. Also, there were a couple of insurance policies that Uncle Bud bought when they first got married. I was the sole beneficiary of those. Ten percent of the estate was given to the Church. There was enough cash in the insurance policies to ensure that we could enjoy our summer cruise, but not much more. I owned the house, but I wasn't ready to sell. I was going to have to find something to do, but I wasn't worried. I was writing again. When I wondered out loud what to do with the house, Kim was the one that came up with the best idea, and just before we left, we helped Johnny Good and his family move in.

Most afternoons were spent on the lake. For a couple of hours each day we would take Bella out and put her though her paces. I used this time to teach Kim the ins and outs of sailing. She picked it up like she had been doing it all her life. On more than one occasion, when we were out by the line in the lake where one can see both the Canadian and American shore, we made love in the cockpit. On one occasion, we inadvertently gave a pretty good show to the crew of a freighter. They blew their horn as they passed. I didn't think they were close enough to see. Kim got embarrassed and swore never to do that again. She lied.

One afternoon, I returned to Earle's place by the canal. I had been having nightmares since the fever broke, and both Johnny and Kim suggested that I return to the scene of the crime. Kim went with me. The old stone house was empty, the property quiet as we pulled into the driveway. There was a for sale sign in the front yard. I listened for any activity. It was eerily quiet, just like the last time I was here. I started to shake a little. I began to ramble. I began to recite. Like a tour guide. Pointing out all the important places. This is where I parked the truck. This is where the police car was. Over there is the barn. The orchard is out back.

I didn't want to go anywhere near the barn, but Kim insisted. We headed back that way, behind the house. As we approached the side of the barn, I stood next to the rusted fuel tank. As I looked around, I could see parts of the orchard and the yard by the house. A rabbit ran around the other side of the barn. A robin picked its way through the grass. It was very peaceful. There was no evidence of the violence of that day. This was Norman Rockwell, not a place of death. Kim and I stood talking.

"I don't want to go in there," I said. I punctuated my statement by sitting on an old cinder block. I leaned back against the oil tank.

"Arn, you've come this far."

"Dickenson," I said, "I never saw that one coming. The first day I met him I thought there was something odd, but I just thought he had a Barney Fife complex. You know. Not sure how to use the power he had. I figured him as goofy, but basically harmless."

"How were you supposed to know," she countered.

"I know. I should have suspected something when he

pulled me over when Aunt Liz and I were coming home from Lockport. Truth is, Aunt Liz put him in his place that day. Like a little kid. That just reinforced my ideas about him. Then that day out in front of the Clintons'..." I shook my head. "Boy was I wrong."

"It's really easy to look back and see things. 20/20 hindsight and all that. Don't beat yourself up. A lot of people knew him and still didn't see this coming."

"I guess," I said. I wasn't sure she was right.

"You know I am," she said as she grabbed my hand. "C'mon. Let's keep moving." I stood, and still holding her hand, we walked around the barn. As we walked to the open doors, I tried to tell her about Dickenson and the song he was whistling. As I remembered it, the song was the theme to the Andy Griffith Show. Kim's only comment was that she always thought Dickenson looked a little like Barney Fife. I had to laugh at that.

I squeezed Kim's hand as we walked into the barn. The posts were still there, the rope that Dickenson used still around the one that held Aunt Liz. Kim asked which one I was tied to, I couldn't speak. I pointed. She walked over and touched the rope. The emotion was too strong, and I walked quickly out of the building.

"Ok," I said. "We've seen it. Let's go."

She hugged me tight. "Show me where you were shot." I just shook my head. Like a little child, she led me. We walked out into the orchard. I wouldn't let go of her hand. I found the ditch that separated the orchard from the canal bank and followed it. After about a hundred yards I stopped. I wasn't sure. Adrenalin was pumping that day, and I was more concerned with staying alive than noting where I was. That, combined with the fact that nature waits for no one, made it hard to find the exact spot. I was about to give up when I noticed an orange flag on a small wire pole sticking out of the tall grass on the other side of a tree. I walked over to it. It appeared to be anonymous in the middle of the orchard, but when we got closer it had 'property of Newport police' printed on the flag. They forgot one. I took this to be the place they found Dickenson's body, and using that as a reference point, I found the tree that I had climbed. Nature had yet been unable to repair the scar created when I ripped the branch off the tree. We could see the bullet hole in the trunk. I said nothing and Kim just hugged me tighter.

I crawled under the tree, and the image of the night spent waiting to die returned with a rush. I remembered the pain. I closed my eyes, trying to shut out the violence of that starry night. I could feel the cold breeze on my face as we stood there. Kim stood silent. I tried to conjure up the meadow. I told Kim about the meadow appearing, and the image of my parents greeting Aunt Liz. I began to cry. Kim said nothing. When I looked at her, she was crying too. She put her arms around me, and we held each other until we stopped. Enough, I decided, and walked out of the orchard. I was walking as fast as my long legs would carry me. Kim had to take two steps to each of my one. I was about six feet ahead of her when we passed the barn again. I vowed never to go back. We sailed the next day.

It was a perfect summer. Bella handled beautifully. The weather was always on our side. Even the odd surprise storms gave us enough warning to find safe harbor. We hit all the ports of interest on the west end of the lake. We went to Cobourg, and Toronto. We stopped at Niagara-On-The-Lake, and as we headed east, again we bounced off the

American coast, stopping at Wilson, and Irondequoit, and we stopped in Sackets Harbor, Alexandria Bay, and Kingston. We wandered through the Thousand Islands. We toured Boldt Castle. We crisscrossed the lake; we got to know the quiet bays and inlets. When we found a secluded spot, we would stay until our supplies ran out, spending each day swimming and making love. On those days, clothing was left in the cabin. We were both getting in better physical shape from all the activity and beginning to turn brown from the sun. The daily workout of swimming and tending to a boat under sail quickly brought me back to good health. As I sit here this morning, I am fifty pounds lighter than when I arrived at Saunders Point. And in the best shape of my life. It was not a weight loss plan that I would recommend though.

The only harbor we avoided was Saunders Point. We passed it several times, in sight of the lighthouse, always deciding that we weren't ready to return. In my mind, I believed that once we did, the summer was over. If it were up to me, I would spend the rest of my life sailing. Head south, maybe all the way to Key West. I am not sure Kim felt the same way. As the summer wore on, she was getting more and more restless. For the past few days, something changed in her behavior. I wanted to know what was bothering her, but I knew from trial and error that if I left her alone, she would come around to it in her own time and tell me. Our first and only fight happened on our second stop in Toronto. I kept pushing her to tell me what was bothering her. She needs to have the time to process information and formulate a thought. As I sit here, I can't remember what the problem was, but the fight lasted two days, and I learned a valuable lesson about my girl.

It was her idea to come to Rochester. She said she wanted a fish fry. I suggested heading to Wilson to the Boat House. She said she was hungry for one from Olee's on the Genesee River. We made for Rochester. It all came to a head last night when we were on Bella at the Rochester Yacht Club. We were overlooking the boat traffic and waiting for the sun to set. We had just returned from O'laughlin's. She had been quiet, all afternoon. She barely said two words at dinner.

I was sitting in the cockpit. I had just opened a Labatt's, wanting to maintain the mild buzz that I had started at the bar. I lit a cigar and was listening to the sounds of the city at night. I leaned back in the cockpit and closed my eyes. My feet were resting on the wheel. It was Saturday night. Across the river, I could hear a rock band playing in one of the bars. Behind them, barely audible, was the sound of traffic going over the bridge. A woman screamed and a man laughed on a boat a few docks over. I closed my eyes and let it all drift in. Kim was reading.

Finally, the time was right. She put her book down and moved in next to me. She grabbed my hand. She finally spoke. "Arn, are you awake?" I just grunted." I talked to Evie the other day..." That woke me up.

"Yeah?" I sat up.

"She wanted to know, was I ever coming back? Or should she post my job in the PennySaver?" She put her book down and looked at me expectantly.

I sat up and looked her in the eyes. "What did you tell her?'

"I said I would be in on Tuesday."

"You mean like the day after the day after tomorrow?" She nodded. "But I'm not ready..."

"Now, Arn. You knew this day was coming. Since the day we left, you knew. You have been sufficiently nursed back to health and are even writing again. My work is done here." She stood and bowed at the waist. "Thank you very much." I couldn't help but laugh. "This summer has been wonderful, but it's time we got back to the real world." She moved over to my side of the boat. She pulled my arm so that it was around her. "You know I'm right."

I kissed her hard. She was right. I knew it but didn't want to admit it. We had been all around this great lake; there weren't too many places we could go where we hadn't been at least once. And it was going to start getting cold. I wasn't sure what I was going to do when it did. I had been a Florida boy for a long time. I guess I could move into a house. I was a little concerned about the idea of winter. I wanted to be ready. Plus, this is shaping up to be a pretty good chunk of writing. I would need to concentrate on it more. It might be a good thing that Kim wasn't around all the time. Still, I wasn't ready.

"That's why you wanted to come to Rochester, isn't it?" My face wasn't six inches away from hers. She nodded and kissed me. "Kim..."

"Arn, this summer has been magical. I have never had such a great time. You, this sturdy old ship, this grand lake." She paused and looked me in the eye. "But it has been a vacation. It has been a holiday. We need to get back to our lives. Evie needs me at the library and..."

"I need to do what I need to do," I interrupted. "Whatever that it is."

"I know you will work it out. I'll help you."

"Can't we just keep sailing? There is so much to think about. Aunt Liz is gone, I don't have a job. I have no money.

Then there is us. It's going to get cold soon. Maybe we could head south. Am I going to live on Bella all winter? When we get back, I have to figure all of that out. As long as we are out here on the lake, I don't have to confront any of it. I don't have to think about it."

"But that's just it. You do have to think about it. We have to think about it. All of it. Even us," she paused and look at me expectantly. "What about us by the way?"

"Ah," I said. "The million-dollar question." I took a sip of beer. She sat up and moved to the other side of the cockpit. Her face began to look like that time when we were in Toronto. I could almost hear the thunder rumbling behind it.

"Just what does that mean mister?"

"What it means is that I don't know. There is so much up in the air right now, I don't really even know where I will be, or what I will be doing next week. How can I talk about a commitment?"

"Who's asking you to?" I just looked at her. She had calmed a little but was still intense.

"Well, I just thought…" I said.

"What?"

"I just thought that when we go back our relationship is going to have to change. We are so good together. I just thought you might want more."

"It will change. I will go home, and you will still be here on Bella. That's what's going to change. We will find you a place to hold up for the winter, and we will work on the rest."

"You're not going to stay here?"

'You gotta be crazy," she laughed. "It's going to get cold. And you aren't going to move in with me. There's not enough room for your stuff. Although I hope you will be spending some of your time there and invite me back to this tub once in a while."

I just shook my head. She was laughing and joking again. I felt like a weight had been lifted from my shoulders. A weight that I didn't even feel until it was gone. In the back of my mind I was beginning to wonder how our relationship was going to fit into the things I needed to get done. I was glad that Kim wanted to still be with me, but I was also glad that she wanted some space too. Things were going to be different, but we would face them all together.

"Ok, we can go back to Saunders Point tomorrow," I said. "Let's make an all-day trip of it. Kind of a swan song. Nice and easy. No hurry." She hugged me.

"That's what I was thinking too." She smiled. "Know what else I'm thinking?" She stood up and went below. She threw her shirt at me as she went. I tossed the butt of my cigar overboard and followed her. As we undressed, there was a familiarity that comes with total knowledge of the other person. I knew her inside and out. I knew what would make her breath quicken, rushing towards the ultimate climax, I knew what to do to slow her down, to make it last. She knew the same things, and sometimes we would drive each other to the edge, only to return, again, and again, in attempt to see who would give in first. It was about a fifty-fifty bet on any given day. Today, I wanted to make it last. I wanted it to be memorable. The air of the cabin was stale and felt like ending. Our summer was ending. Our life together was going to take on a new dimension. I wanted to make sure that she didn't forget about old Arn.

We were lying in bed when the alarm from the GPS told me it was time to change tack. I slipped out, naked, and changed course setting the autopilot for the Saunders Point Lighthouse. It would be about an hour before we would see the light house, so I went back down to the cabin. Kim was asleep so I grabbed a Labatt's and headed back out to my laptop.

THIRTY-EIGHT

It's about 6:30 Sunday night. The wind has died out. The lake is flat. The sails have been stowed and Bella's little ten horse is moving us towards the piers at a slow, but steady pace. Kim is at the wheel, wanting one last shift, and I am trying to finish this narrative. The notes that I started when this all began to help me to try and make sense of it all have turned into more. A collection of experiences, thoughts and conjectures that look like they might turn into my next project. It's a crazy story. I am not sure anyone would buy it as fiction. But I am going to try. Maybe change a name here or there. Maybe a location. It feels good to be writing again. We will be docked at the marina in less than thirty minutes. Kim will probably go home. I am going to miss having her here all the time, but at the same time I think it will be good for us.

I am racing to finish up these thoughts before we get to the channel. I find that I have one more thing to add. I have not been completely honest, and I need to clear the air. As close as we have become, I have a secret that even Kim doesn't know. My statement that I would never go back to Earle's house was not completely true. I did go back. The day we left, Kim when to Newport to get some groceries and have lunch with Evie. After I was sure that I would not run into her, I hopped into Aunt Liz's car, and taking all the back roads, crossed the canal bridge, and pulled into the driveway of Earle's now empty house. The 'for sale' sign in the front yard squeaked as it swung gently in the breeze. I pulled up around the house, where Dickenson had parked the squad car. It was almost out of sight from the road. I parked in the same spot. I didn't want to be disturbed. I walked around the house and stood by the barn.

See, there is something that had been bothering me. Ever since the fever broke, I have been dreaming about the barn. This barn. In my dream, I am always walking around the outside of the barn, around the old fuel tank. Every time, I kneel down by the tank, listening for Dickenson. I hear him whistling. I want to run. When I stand up, I wake up. One morning, when I woke up, I remembered a specific detail about the fuel tank. There was an access panel on the side of the tank, and the old rusted bolts that held it on were burred. New steel sticking out against the rust. Like someone used a pair of pliers instead of a wrench. I wanted to see if the real tank had an access panel in it, and if the real bolts were burred.

It took all my strength that day to walk back out to the barn. I expected Dickenson to come out from behind the barn, whistling, with his gun blazing. Picking me off again. I kept going. I got to the tank. Sure enough, there was an access panel. The bolts were beginning to rust again, but clearly, they had been tampered with. They were burred beyond the ability to put a wrench on them.

I pulled the Vise grips that I had brought from a little toolbox I keep on Bella and tried one. It came loose. There were six in all, and they all came out with surprising ease. I opened the tank and stuck my hand in. There were six plastic bags in the bottom of the tank. Each filled with wrapped packs of twenty-dollar bills. I counted one. The first stack was one thousand dollars. There were twenty more in the first bag. The other five also had stacks of twenties, some had twenty-some less. When I finished emptying the bags, I had one hundred stacks. I had found Earle's stash. He had died not telling Dickenson where it was. I smiled at the thought that Dickenson had walked by this tank several times that day. Earle had gotten the last laugh after all. I put the panel back on the tank and rubbed dirt on the bolts to make them look rusted. I was just putting my mattress back on the bed when Kim returned. The toolbox was full now. The money fit in there perfectly. All wrapped up in their original plastic bags. I know, I probably should turn it in. At least, I probably should tell Kim about it. Maybe someday. The way I see it, the money is compensation. I earned it. Besides, who would I return it to? I will have to think about it. Until then, I will just enjoy life a little more for a while. Kim just called me back to reality. We are passing the breakwater. She has slowed down, and I am going to close the laptop.

"Kim, you just passed the river." I looked at her questioningly.

"I know," she said and pointed. "The sun is about to set. Let's stay out here. We can eat dinner and watch it go down."

"Great idea." I smiled and kissed her. We pulled past the piers and up a little closer to shore. We turned the boat so that the cockpit was facing the sun, and I secured her with two anchors. One off the bow, and one off the stern. We weren't going anywhere. There was nothing but lake between us and the view. Kim moved down the stairs to get things ready. I set up the grill and had a fire going just as she reemerged with a plate of strip steaks, and a couple of gin and tonics.

"To a great idea," I said as we clinked glasses. She took a big sip and went back to the galley. I put the steaks on the hot grill and lit a cigar.

We sat in the cockpit. The evening sky put on a great show as we ate. Spinach salad with a homemade vinaigrette, and rosemary potatoes, that she had wrapped in foil and I had roasted on the grill.

"This is what we ate that first night on the boat," I said.

"Yep." She nodded. "And this." She brought out a bottle of Yellow Tail Shiraz. "I wanted this meal to be special. As soon as we cruise inside that channel, our vacation ends and our real lives begin. You ready?"

"Ugh, Not really." I said, with a mock frown. I poured the wine. "Actually, I think I am. I've been thinking since last night. I never said thank you for all that you did for me. Don't think I ever said I love you either, but I do. Us together, I know it will all come together somehow."

"Arn," she just smiled. Her eyes softened, and I saw a small tear escape from one. "I love you too. I wanted to say it a couple of times, but it just didn't seem like the right time."

She hugged me." As for the thank you, I am glad you are better, but if you ever try to put me through that again, the next time you get shot by a crazed killer, you are on your own."

"Kim," I started.

"Shut up and pass the potatoes," she said and laughed. That was the end of that. "Besides, I'm kind of excited to see where it's all going to go."

We didn't say much as we cleared dinner away. Lost in our own thoughts, we were silent as we sat together watching the sky turn from yellow to orange then to red. The sun looked like a glowing ball sinking into the lake. When the colors finally faded, and the sun was just a sliver on the horizon, we looked at each other.

"It's time," I said. "You want to do the honors?"

"Oh yeah," she said, as she moved to the wheel and started the motor. I hoisted the anchors and set to coiling the rope and stowing them in their bunkers as we started moving towards the piers. It seemed like a lifetime ago that I stood on that pier, alone. Wondering why I even came to Saunders Point. I jumped into the cockpit and looked at Kim. She was smiling. I felt that same sentimental tightness in my throat as we passed the lighthouse. "Welcome Home," it was saying. This time, I was glad.

ABOUT ATMOSPHERE PRESS

Atmosphere Press is an independent, full-service publisher for excellent books in all genres and for all audiences. Learn more about what we do at atmospherepress.com.

We encourage you to check out some of Atmosphere's latest releases, which are available at Amazon.com and via order from your local bookstore:

Itsuki, a novel by Zach MacDonald

A Surprising Measure of Subliminal Sadness, short stories by Sue Powers

Saint Lazarus Day, short stories by R. Conrad Speer

My Father's Eyes, a novel by Michael Osborne

The Lower Canyons, a novel by John Manuel

Shiftless, a novel by Anthony C. Murphy

The Escapist, a novel by Karahn Washington

Gerbert's Book, a novel by Bob Mustin

Tree One, a novel by Fred Caron

Connie Undone, a novel by Kristine Brown

A Cage Called Freedom, a novel by Paul P.S. Berg

Shining in Infinity, a novel by Charles McIntyre

Buildings Without Murders, a novel by Dan Gutstein

ABOUT THE AUTHOR

Kevin has lived in the shadow of the fictional village of Newport and worked as a carpenter for most of his life. His first publication, *Vague Path*, a collection of original poems, was created while still 'in the field.' He continued to write while trying to find his place in the world. When life demanded that he make a change, he developed his creativity and love of words into a career in teaching, and creative writing. That lead him to SUNY Brockport and a master's degree. *Lost and Found* is his first venture into the world of fiction. He is currently teaching writing at Genesee Community College and has many writing projects in the works. Kevin has three children and two grandchildren. He currently lives a stone's throw away from the Historic Erie Canal with his wife, and step-daughter.